Greek Mythology for Beginners:

Enchanting and Timeless Tales of Gods, Heroes, and Monsters. Unveil the Secrets of Ancient Legends and Explore the Stories that Defined History.

ETHAN CRAFTWELL

Welcome to 'Greek Mythology for Beginners.'

As a sign of our appreciation for your interest in this fascinating hobby, we've prepared something extra just for you.

The QR code below is your gateway to downloading our exclusive e-book featuring 10 divine recipes inspired by Greek myths and gods.

TABLE OF CONTENTS

INTRODUCTION

Welcome to the World of Greek Mythology

Welcome to the enchanting world of Greek Mythology! Imagine a universe filled with powerful gods, valiant heroes, and mythical creatures. This is a world where the impossible becomes possible, and the ordinary transforms into the extraordinary.

Greek mythology is not just a collection of old stories; it's a vibrant tapestry that has shaped literature, art, and culture for centuries.

But why should you dive into these ancient tales? Well, Greek mythology offers a unique lens through which we can understand the ancient world and, surprisingly, our modern lives too. The themes of love, power, jealousy, and heroism are as relevant today as they were thousands of years ago. Through these stories, we connect with universal human experiences, bridging the gap between past and present.

The Allure of Ancient Myths

What makes Greek mythology so alluring? Perhaps it's the sheer drama of the tales. Think of the epic battles of the Trojan War, the trials of Odysseus, or the tragic love story of Orpheus and Eurydice. These stories captivate us with their blend of adventure, romance, and moral lessons.

Greek myths also serve as a mirror, reflecting the values and beliefs of ancient Greek society. They provide insights into how the Greeks understood the world, their gods, and themselves. For instance, the myth of Prometheus, who defied Zeus to bring fire to humanity, speaks volumes about the Greek view on innovation and defiance.

Moreover, the gods and goddesses of Greek mythology are richly complex characters. They are powerful yet flawed, majestic yet petty. Zeus, the king of the gods, rules with authority but is often driven by personal desires. Athena, the goddess of wisdom, embodies intellect and strategy, while Ares, the god of war, represents brute strength and chaos. These divine beings reflect the multifaceted nature of humanity, making their stories both relatable and endlessly fascinating.

How to Use This Book

This book is your guide to exploring the vast landscape of Greek mythology. Here's how to make the most of it:

1. **Start with the Basics**: If you're new to Greek mythology, begin with the introductory sections. They provide a foundation, introducing key gods, goddesses, and major myths. This will give you a solid grounding in the essential stories and characters.

2. **Dive into the Details**: Once you're familiar with the basics, explore the thematic sections. These delve deeper into specific myths, analyzing their meanings and cultural significance. You'll find detailed retellings and insights into how these stories have been interpreted through the ages.

3. **Connect with the Characters**: Greek mythology is rich with compelling characters. Use the character profiles to get to know the gods, heroes, and monsters. Understanding their personalities and motivations will enhance your appreciation of the myths.

4. **Engage with the Myths**: Reflect on how these ancient stories resonate with your own life. Consider their moral and philosophical lessons. The myths often raise questions about fate, morality, and human nature that are still relevant today.

5. **Visual Exploration**: Enjoy the illustrations throughout the book. These bring the myths to life, helping you visualize the gods and their exploits. High-quality images of ancient artworks and modern interpretations will enrich your understanding and enjoyment.

6. **Interactive Elements**: Take advantage of interactive elements such as quizzes and discussion prompts.. These are designed to deepen your engagement and make learning about Greek mythology a fun and immersive experience.

This book aims to be a journey into a world where the boundaries between reality and imagination blur, inviting you to explore, reflect, and enjoy the timeless tales of Greek mythology. So, turn the page, and let the adventure begin!

CHAPTER 1:
THE BIRTH OF THE GODS

1.1 CHAOS AND CREATION MYTHS

Greek mythology begins with Chaos, an expansive, formless void that existed before the creation of the universe. This primordial chaos was not merely empty space; it was a potent mixture of the elements, the raw material from which everything else would emerge. Imagine a swirling, dark abyss brimming with potential but lacking form or order. From this chaotic void sprang the first primordial deities, representing fundamental aspects of existence.

The Primordial Deities

Chaos gave birth to several primordial entities: Gaia (Earth), Tartarus (the Underworld), Eros (Love), Erebus (Darkness), and Nyx (Night). Each of these entities played a crucial role in the creation of the world and the establishment of order. Gaia, the Earth, emerged as a solid foundation from the swirling chaos. She was both a physical and a maternal presence, embodying the planet and nurturing life. Gaia alone bore Uranus (the Sky), who enveloped her entirely. Their union produced the first generation of Titans, the Cyclopes, and the Hecatoncheires (Hundred-Handed Ones).

Gaia and Uranus

Gaia and Uranus's union was fruitful, producing powerful offspring that embodied raw elemental forces. However, Uranus, fearing the power of his children, imprisoned them deep within Gaia. This caused Gaia great pain and set the stage for a rebellion. With Gaia's encouragement, her son Cronus ambushed Uranus. Using a sickle provided by Gaia, Cronus castrated his father, and from Uranus's blood sprang the Erinyes (Furies), the Giants, and the Meliae (Nymphs). The severed genitals, cast into the sea, gave rise to Aphrodite, the goddess of love and beauty. This act of defiance and creation from violence is a recurring theme in Greek mythology, reflecting the turbulent nature of the cosmos.

The Reign of Cronus

With Uranus overthrown, Cronus and his siblings, the Titans, assumed control of the cosmos. Cronus became the ruler, but like his father, he feared his children. Prophecy warned that one of his offspring would overthrow him. To prevent this, Cronus swallowed each of his children at birth. This gruesome act highlights the recurring theme of parental fear and the inevitable cycle of succession in Greek mythology.

Rhea, Cronus's sister and wife, grew weary of losing her children. When she gave birth to Zeus, she devised a plan to save him. Rhea hid the newborn in a cave on Mount Ida in Crete, giving Cronus a stone wrapped in swaddling clothes, which he swallowed, believing it was his son. This act of deception was crucial, setting the stage for the rise of the Olympian gods.

The Rise of Zeus

Zeus grew up in secret, nurtured by nymphs and guarded by the Kouretes, warriors who clashed their weapons to drown out his cries. When he reached adulthood, Zeus sought to free his siblings. With the help of Metis, the goddess of wisdom, he concocted a potion that forced Cronus to vomit up his children: Hestia, Demeter, Hera, Hades, and Poseidon. This dramatic liberation marks the beginning of the struggle for cosmic supremacy between the Titans and the Olympians.

The Titanomachy

The battle between the Olympians and the Titans, known as the Titanomachy, was a prolonged and epic conflict that lasted for ten years. The Olympians, with Zeus as their leader, sought to establish a new order in the cosmos. The Cyclopes and the Hecatoncheires, whom Zeus freed from their subterranean prison, played crucial roles in the Olympian victory. The Cyclopes gifted Zeus with thunderbolts, Poseidon with a trident, and Hades with a helm of darkness, tools that would be crucial in their victory.

The New Order

With the Titans defeated, Zeus established a new order. He and his brothers drew lots to divide the realms of the universe: Zeus claimed the sky, Poseidon the sea, and Hades the underworld. The earth was left for all to share. This division marked the beginning of the Olympian era, characterized by a new generation of gods who would interact with mortals in myriad ways, shaping their destinies and the world around them.

Symbolism and Interpretation

The creation myths of Greek mythology are rich with symbolic meaning. Chaos represents the unknown and unformed potential, while Gaia and Uranus symbolize the Earth and Sky, fundamental components of the natural world.

The cyclical nature of power, with each generation overthrowing the previous one, reflects the Greeks' understanding of change and succession in both nature and human affairs.

Cronus's act of swallowing his children underscores the inevitability of fate and the futility of trying to escape it, a recurring theme in Greek mythology. The eventual rise of Zeus and the establishment of the Olympian order signify the triumph of a new era, bringing a sense of structure and stability to the cosmos.

These myths served not only as explanations for the origins of the world and its natural phenomena but also as reflections of human experience and psychology. They provided ancient Greeks with a framework to understand their place in the universe, the forces that governed their lives, and the complexities of human nature.

The Role of the Primordial Deities

The primordial deities play a foundational role in Greek mythology. Chaos, as the source of everything, embodies the infinite possibilities of creation. Gaia, as the earth mother, represents fertility and life, while Uranus, the sky, signifies the overarching presence that influences and interacts with the earth.

Tartarus, the deep abyss used as a dungeon of torment, underscores the existence of a counterbalance to the heavens—an underworld that plays a crucial role in later myths. Eros, the force of love and attraction, is essential for the procreation and continuation of life. Erebus and Nyx, embodiments of darkness and night, represent the inevitable presence of shadow and mystery in the world.

Cultural Impact and Legacy

These creation myths have left an indelible mark on Western culture. They influenced not only the religious practices of the ancient Greeks but also their art, literature, and philosophy. The themes of creation, rebellion, and order found in these myths resonate through the works of Hesiod and Homer, two of the most important literary figures in Greek history. These myths provided a narrative structure for understanding the world and humanity's place within it, laying the groundwork for Western thought and storytelling.

The chaos and creation myths of Greek mythology offer a rich tapestry of stories that explain the origins of the world and the gods. They explore themes of creation, power, rebellion, and order, reflecting the complexities of human experience. Through these myths, the ancient Greeks sought to understand their universe, imparting lessons that continue to resonate with us today. These timeless stories invite us to ponder the mysteries of existence and the forces that shape our world.

1.2 THE TITANS AND THEIR REIGN

Following the chaotic beginnings of the universe and the establishment of primordial deities, the narrative of Greek mythology transitions to the era of the Titans. The Titans were the children of Gaia (Earth) and Uranus (Sky), and they played a pivotal role in the early mythological history. These powerful beings governed the cosmos during a time often referred to as the Golden Age, a period marked by peace and prosperity.

The Rise of the Titans

After Cronus, the youngest of the Titans, overthrew his father Uranus with the help of his mother Gaia, he assumed control of the universe. This act of rebellion not only signified the end of Uranus's tyrannical rule but also marked the beginning of a new era under the reign of the Titans. Cronus released his Titan siblings from their confinement, and together, they established their dominion over the cosmos.

Cronus, now the supreme ruler, married his sister Rhea. The Titans, each representing various aspects of nature and human experience, included notable figures such as Oceanus (the Ocean), Tethys (the nurturing mother), Hyperion (the Sun), Theia (sight and the bright sky), Coeus (intelligence), Phoebe (prophecy), Mnemosyne (memory), and others. Their reign was characterized by stability and abundance, a stark contrast to the chaos that preceded them.

The Golden Age

The period of Titan rule is often described as the Golden Age. During this time, humanity lived in harmony with the gods, free from the toil and suffering that would later characterize human existence. The earth provided abundantly without the need for labor, and peace prevailed across the land. This idyllic era is a common motif in mythologies worldwide, representing an idealized past before the advent of human frailty and corruption.

The Titans maintained this utopian order through their control over various elements and forces of nature. Hyperion and Theia, for instance, were responsible for the celestial bodies, ensuring the regular cycles of day and night. Oceanus and Tethys governed the waters, while Mnemosyne preserved the collective memory of the gods. Each Titan played a vital role in maintaining the balance and harmony of the world.

The Fear of Prophecy

Despite the prosperity of the Golden Age, Cronus was haunted by a prophecy that one of his children would overthrow him, just as he had overthrown Uranus. This fear drove Cronus to a drastic and cruel measure: he decided to swallow each of his children as soon as they were born. Thus, Hestia, Demeter, Hera, Hades, and Poseidon were consumed by their father, preventing them from growing up to challenge his authority.

Rhea, devastated by the loss of her children, devised a plan to save her youngest, Zeus. When Zeus was born, Rhea hid him in a cave on the island of Crete, giving Cronus a stone wrapped in swaddling clothes instead. Cronus, unaware of the deception, swallowed the stone, believing it to be his newborn son. This act of cunning by Rhea set the stage for the eventual downfall of Cronus and the Titans.

The Overthrow of the Titans

Zeus grew up in secret, nurtured by nymphs and protected by the Kouretes, who clashed their weapons to drown out his cries. Upon reaching maturity, Zeus resolved to rescue his siblings and overthrow Cronus. With the help of Metis, the goddess of wisdom, Zeus prepared a potion that forced Cronus to regurgitate the swallowed children. Reunited, Zeus and his siblings prepared for a monumental battle against the Titans.

This conflict, known as the Titanomachy, lasted for ten years and involved fierce battles that shook the very foundations of the earth. The Olympians, led by Zeus, allied with the Cyclopes and the Hecatoncheires, whom Zeus had freed from their imprisonment by Uranus. The Cyclopes provided Zeus with his iconic thunderbolts, Poseidon with his trident, and Hades with his helm of darkness. These powerful weapons were instrumental in the Olympian victory.

The Aftermath of the Titanomachy

With the Titans defeated, Zeus and his allies established a new order. The defeated Titans were confined to Tartarus, a deep abyss within the earth, ensuring they could no longer threaten the stability of the cosmos. Some Titans, such as Prometheus and Epimetheus, were spared due to their neutrality or contributions to the Olympians' cause. This transition from Titan rule to Olympian dominance marked a significant shift in Greek mythology, as the gods now known as the Olympians took center stage.

The era of the Titans, though marked by their eventual downfall, laid the groundwork for the Olympian age. It was a time of both great harmony and intense conflict, reflecting the dual nature of the cosmos and the perpetual struggle between order and chaos. The myths of the Titans and their reign continue to captivate us, offering insights into themes of power, rebellion, and the cyclical nature of time and authority.

Symbolism and Cultural Impact

The reign of the Titans symbolizes a primordial era, a time when the universe was governed by elemental forces and primal beings. Their eventual overthrow by the Olympians represents the progression from chaos to order, from a more primitive understanding of the world to a more structured and complex one. This mythological shift mirrors human development, reflecting the evolution of society and the emergence of more sophisticated systems of governance and belief.

In art and literature, the Titans have been depicted as powerful and often tragic figures, embodying both the grandeur and the inevitable decline of the ancient order. Their stories have inspired countless works, from classical sculptures and paintings to modern adaptations in books and films. The enduring appeal of these myths lies in their rich symbolism and the universal themes they explore.

Legacy of the Titans

The legacy of the Titans is profound, as their myths form the foundation upon which much of Greek mythology is built. Their stories provide context for the rise of the Olympian gods and the complex relationships and conflicts that define the mythological narrative. The Titans' influence extends beyond mythology, shaping cultural and philosophical thought throughout history.

The era of the Titans represents a crucial chapter in Greek mythology, characterized by the rise and fall of powerful deities who governed the cosmos before the advent of the Olympian gods. Their reign, marked by both harmony and conflict, set the stage for the dramatic events that would follow, shaping the mythological landscape and leaving an enduring legacy that continues to fascinate and inspire.

1.3 THE RISE OF THE OLYMPIAN GODS

The rise of the Olympian gods marks a pivotal transformation in Greek mythology, heralding a new era of divine rule and cosmic order. This transition from the age of the Titans to the reign of the Olympians is characterized by epic battles, cunning strategies, and the establishment of a pantheon that would profoundly influence Western culture and thought.

Zeus's Secret Childhood

The story begins with Zeus, the youngest son of the Titan Cronus and his wife Rhea. Cronus, having overthrown his own father Uranus, feared a prophecy that foretold his downfall at the hands of one of his children. To prevent this, he swallowed each of his offspring at birth: Hestia, Demeter, Hera, Hades, and Poseidon. However, when Rhea bore Zeus, she decided to save him from this grim fate. She secretly gave birth to Zeus in a cave on the island of Crete and handed Cronus a stone wrapped in swaddling clothes, which he promptly swallowed.

Zeus was raised in secrecy, nurtured by nymphs and protected by the Kouretes, warriors who clashed their weapons to drown out his cries. This clandestine upbringing was crucial, as it allowed Zeus to grow into a powerful and cunning god, destined to challenge his father.

The Liberation of Zeus's Siblings

Upon reaching maturity, Zeus sought to rescue his siblings and fulfill the prophecy. With the aid of Metis, the goddess of wisdom and cunning, he devised a plan to overthrow Cronus. Metis prepared a potion that would cause Cronus to regurgitate the swallowed gods. Zeus cleverly disguised himself as an Olympian cupbearer and served the potion to Cronus, who unwittingly consumed it. The potion worked, and Cronus vomited up Hestia, Demeter, Hera,

Hades, and Poseidon, who emerged fully grown and eager to join Zeus in his rebellion.

The Titanomachy: War with the Titans

The liberation of his siblings marked the beginning of the Titanomachy, a ten-year war between the Olympian gods and the Titans. This epic battle was fought on a grand scale, with both sides wielding immense power and influence over the natural world. The Olympians, led by Zeus, were determined to establish a new order, while the Titans, led by Cronus, fought to maintain their dominion.

Zeus and his allies sought additional support to tip the scales in their favor. They descended into Tartarus and freed the Cyclopes and the Hecatoncheires, ancient and formidable beings imprisoned by Uranus. Grateful for their liberation, the Cyclopes gifted Zeus with thunderbolts, Poseidon with a trident, and Hades with a helm of darkness. These powerful weapons played a crucial role in the Olympians' strategy, enhancing their combat capabilities significantly.

Key Battles and Turning Points

Throughout the Titanomachy, numerous battles raged across the cosmos, shaking the foundations of the earth and sky. The Hecatoncheires, with their hundred hands, hurled massive boulders at the Titans, while Zeus unleashed his thunderbolts, creating devastating storms. Poseidon's trident caused earthquakes and tsunamis, and Hades used his helm of darkness to move unseen and strike at critical moments.

One of the pivotal battles occurred on Mount Othrys, the stronghold of the Titans. Here, the combined forces of the Olympians and their allies launched a relentless assault. The Olympians' superior strategy and the raw power of their newfound allies gradually overwhelmed the Titans. Cronus and his brothers fought valiantly, but they could not withstand the coordinated onslaught led by Zeus.

The Fall of the Titans

The decisive moment came when Zeus, with a final, mighty throw of his thunderbolt, struck Cronus down. The defeat of Cronus symbolized the end of the Titans' reign and the beginning of a new era under the Olympian gods. The Titans were cast into Tartarus, where they were imprisoned for eternity, ensuring they could no longer threaten the new order.

However, not all Titans met this grim fate. Some, like Prometheus and Epimetheus, who had not actively opposed the Olympians, were spared and allowed to roam free. Prometheus, in particular, would play a crucial role in later myths, especially in the creation and development of humanity.

Establishing the Olympian Order

With the Titans defeated, Zeus and his siblings established their rule from Mount Olympus, the highest peak in Greece, which became the divine residence of the gods. Zeus, as the ruler of the sky, assumed the position of the supreme deity. He was responsible for law, order, and justice among gods and mortals alike. Poseidon took dominion over the seas, wielding his trident to control oceans and waterways. Hades became the ruler of the underworld, governing the realm of the dead with his helm of darkness.

The other Olympian gods also took on important roles. Hera, as Zeus's wife, became the goddess of marriage and childbirth. Demeter, the goddess of agriculture, ensured the fertility of the earth and the cycles of the seasons. Hestia, the goddess of hearth and home, represented domesticity and family. Together, they formed a powerful pantheon that governed all aspects of the natural and human worlds.

The Olympian Legacy

The rise of the Olympian gods brought a new order to the cosmos, characterized by a balance between chaos and order, power and justice. The myths surrounding their rise are rich with themes of rebellion, familial conflict, and the establishment of new authority. These stories not only explain the origins of the gods and their dominion over various realms but also reflect the ancient Greeks' views on power, legitimacy, and the cyclical nature of time.

The Olympian gods, each with their unique personalities and domains, became central figures in Greek religion and culture. Their myths were told and retold, shaping the beliefs and values of ancient Greek society. The stories of their adventures, conflicts, and interactions with mortals provided moral lessons and cultural touchstones that continue to resonate in literature, art, and philosophy.

Symbolism and Interpretation

The rise of the Olympian gods can be seen as a symbolic reflection of societal evolution. The transition from the rule of the Titans to the Olympians represents the shift from an older, more chaotic order to a structured and governed system. This mirrors the development of human civilizations, where emerging societies establish laws, hierarchies, and cultural norms to replace more primitive states of existence.

Moreover, the struggles and conflicts among the gods illustrate fundamental aspects of the human condition, such as the desire for power, the complexity of familial relationships, and the inevitability of change. Zeus's journey from a hidden child to the ruler of the cosmos emphasizes themes of destiny, resilience, and the rightful ascension of new leadership.

The rise of the Olympian gods is a cornerstone of Greek mythology, marking the transition from the age of the Titans to a new divine order. This chapter in the mythological narrative is filled with dramatic conflicts, strategic alliances, and the establishment of a powerful pantheon that would shape the religious and cultural landscape of ancient Greece. The legacy of the Olympians endures, offering timeless stories that continue to captivate and inspire us with their profound insights into the nature of power, order, and the human experience.

1.4 PROMETHEUS AND THE CREATION OF MAN

In Greek mythology, the figure of Prometheus stands out as a symbol of defiance, intelligence, and compassion. His story is intertwined with the creation of humanity and the bestowal of gifts that would define the human experience. Prometheus, a Titan whose name means "forethought," played a crucial role in shaping the destiny of mankind and defying the will of Zeus, the king of the gods.

Prometheus and the Titans

Prometheus was one of the Titans, the children of Gaia and Uranus. Unlike many of his brethren, Prometheus sided with Zeus during the Titanomachy, the great war between the Titans and the Olympians. This allegiance to Zeus initially placed Prometheus in a favorable position, but his sympathy for humanity would eventually lead to a profound conflict with the Olympian ruler.

The Creation of Man

According to the myth, after the Olympians established their dominion, Prometheus took it upon himself to create mankind. He fashioned humans out of clay, imbuing them with form and life. In some versions of the myth, Athena, the goddess of wisdom, breathed life into the clay figures, animating them with her divine breath. This act of creation was a collaborative effort between Prometheus and Athena, symbolizing the union of craft and intellect.

Prometheus shaped humanity with care, making them upright like the gods, and endowed them with the capacity for reason and intelligence. However, despite his best efforts, the newly created humans were weak and vulnerable compared to the mighty Olympian gods. They lacked the means to protect themselves from the elements and the beasts that roamed the earth.

The Gift of Fire

Moved by the plight of his creations, Prometheus resolved to empower humanity. He decided to steal fire from the gods and give it to mankind. Fire, a symbol of knowledge, technology, and civilization, was zealously guarded by the gods, particularly by Hephaestus, the god of fire and forge. Prometheus's decision to steal fire was a bold and dangerous act, as it directly defied Zeus's command.

Prometheus ascended Mount Olympus under the cover of night, approached the forge of Hephaestus, and took a glowing ember.

Concealing the fire in a hollow fennel stalk, he descended back to the mortal world and presented the precious gift to humanity. With fire, humans could now cook their food, warm themselves, craft tools, and ward off wild animals. This monumental gift marked the beginning of human progress and civilization.

The Wrath of Zeus

Zeus was furious when he discovered Prometheus's theft. He viewed the act not only as a direct defiance of his authority but also as a disruption of the natural order he had established. In Zeus's eyes, humanity was meant to be weak and dependent on the gods, not empowered and self-sufficient. The gift of fire had elevated humans closer to the divine, blurring the lines between mortals and gods.

To punish Prometheus for his transgression, Zeus devised a cruel and eternal torment. Prometheus was bound to a rock on Mount Caucasus, where an eagle, the emblem of Zeus, would visit him every day to feast on his liver. Each night, his liver would regenerate, ensuring that his suffering was endless. This punishment symbolized the price of defiance and the relentless nature of divine retribution.

The Creation of Pandora

Zeus's vengeance did not stop with Prometheus. He also sought to punish humanity for accepting the stolen fire. To achieve this, he ordered Hephaestus to create the first woman, Pandora, out of clay. Each god endowed her with a unique trait: beauty, charm, cunning, and curiosity. Zeus presented Pandora to Epimetheus, Prometheus's brother, who accepted her despite Prometheus's warnings about accepting gifts from Zeus.

Pandora brought with her a jar (often mistranslated as a box) containing all the evils of the world. Driven by curiosity, Pandora eventually opened the jar, releasing diseases, plagues, sorrow, and death into the world. Only hope remained inside the jar, offering a small respite from the newfound suffering. This myth explains the origin of human suffering and the dual nature of hope as both a comfort and a reminder of potential despair.

The Legacy of Prometheus

Despite his eternal punishment, Prometheus remained a symbol of enduring defiance and the quest for knowledge. His actions underscored the values of foresight, sacrifice, and the relentless pursuit of progress. Prometheus's name became synonymous with the human spirit's unyielding desire to overcome adversity and seek enlightenment.

In later myths, Prometheus's torment came to an end through the intervention of Heracles (Hercules), the great hero. As part of his Twelve Labors, Heracles killed the eagle that tormented Prometheus and freed the Titan from his chains. This act of liberation not only highlighted Heracles's strength and heroism but also symbolized the triumph of perseverance and justice.

Symbolism and Interpretation

Prometheus's story is rich with symbolic meanings and interpretations. His creation of humanity from clay reflects the belief in a divine origin of human life and the intimate connection between gods and mortals. The gift of fire represents the dawn of civilization, the power of knowledge, and the transformative impact of technology.

Prometheus's defiance against Zeus illustrates the tension between authority and rebellion, the consequences of challenging the status quo, and the inevitable clash between innovation and tradition. His punishment highlights the theme of eternal suffering and the price of wisdom, while his eventual liberation by Heracles signifies the enduring hope for redemption and the victory of resilience.

Cultural Impact

The myth of Prometheus has resonated through the ages, inspiring countless works of art, literature, and philosophy. In ancient Greece, he was revered as a culture hero and a benefactor of humanity. In the modern era, Prometheus's legacy continues to influence thinkers, writers, and artists who explore themes of defiance, creativity, and human potential.

Prometheus's story has been interpreted in various ways, from a cautionary tale about the dangers of hubris to an inspiring narrative about the pursuit of knowledge and the spirit of resistance. His enduring legacy serves as a reminder of the complex relationship between gods and mortals, the power of foresight and innovation, and the unbreakable will of the human spirit.

Prometheus's role in the creation of man and the gift of fire is a foundational myth in Greek mythology, embodying the themes of creation, defiance, suffering, and redemption. His story offers profound insights into the nature of humanity, the pursuit of knowledge, and the enduring struggle for freedom and progress. Through Prometheus, we see the reflection of our own aspirations and the timeless quest to illuminate the darkness with the light of understanding.

1.5 THE MYTH OF PANDORA'S BOX

The myth of Pandora's Box is one of the most enduring and profound tales in Greek mythology. It offers a poignant explanation for the existence of evil and suffering in the world while also highlighting the complexities of human nature. This story centers around Pandora, the first woman created by the gods, and her pivotal role in introducing misfortune to humanity.

The Creation of Pandora

After Prometheus defied Zeus by giving fire to humanity, Zeus decided to punish both Prometheus and mankind. While Prometheus was condemned to eternal torment, Zeus concocted a plan to bring suffering to humans. He commanded Hephaestus, the god of blacksmiths and craftsmanship, to create the first woman from clay. This woman, Pandora, whose name means "all-gifted," was endowed with various traits by the gods.

Each deity contributed to Pandora's creation: Aphrodite gave her beauty, Athena bestowed her with wisdom and skill, Hermes granted her cunning and charm, and Zeus himself infused her with curiosity and a sense of mischief. The gods dressed her in magnificent garments and adorned her with precious jewels, making her irresistibly attractive. This multifaceted gift would ultimately lead to humanity's downfall.

Pandora's Arrival

Zeus presented Pandora to Epimetheus, the brother of Prometheus. Despite Prometheus's warnings never to accept gifts from Zeus, Epimetheus was enchanted by Pandora's beauty and grace and accepted her as his wife. Along with Pandora, Zeus sent a mysterious jar (often mistranslated as a box) as a wedding gift, but with a strict instruction that it should never be opened.

For a time, Pandora and Epimetheus lived happily. However, the curiosity that Zeus had instilled in Pandora began to grow. She could not resist the urge to discover what lay inside the jar. This insatiable curiosity, a quintessentially human trait, was both a gift and a curse.

The Opening of the Box

One day, Pandora's curiosity overcame her, and she decided to open the jar. As she lifted the lid, all the evils contained within it—disease, sorrow, death, and myriad other forms of suffering—escaped and spread throughout the world. These calamities, once unleashed, could not be recaptured, marking the end of the Golden Age of humanity, a time of peace and prosperity.

Horrified by what she had done, Pandora quickly closed the jar, but it was too late. The evils had already escaped. Only one thing remained inside: Elpis, the spirit of Hope. In some versions of the myth, Hope is depicted as a small, fragile figure, suggesting that even amidst overwhelming adversity, hope remains a delicate but essential part of the human condition.

Symbolism and Themes

The myth of Pandora's Box is rich with symbolism and explores several themes central to Greek mythology and human existence:

1. **Curiosity and Consequence**: Pandora's curiosity reflects a fundamental aspect of human nature—the desire to explore the unknown. While curiosity drives discovery and progress, it also carries the risk of unforeseen consequences. The myth suggests that the pursuit of knowledge and understanding can lead to both enlightenment and suffering.
2. **The Nature of Evil**: The evils that escaped from Pandora's jar represent the myriad challenges and hardships that humans face. These include physical ailments, emotional distress, and existential threats. The myth provides a narrative framework for understanding the origin of suffering in the world.
3. **Hope as a Solace**: The presence of Hope at the bottom of the jar signifies that even in the darkest times, hope persists. This duality of hope and despair is a central theme, highlighting the resilience of the human spirit. Hope offers a glimmer of optimism and the possibility of overcoming adversity.
4. **Divine Retribution and Justice**: The myth also underscores the theme of divine retribution. Zeus's punishment of humanity through Pandora's actions reflects

the gods' power to influence human fate and the consequences of defying divine authority.

Cultural Impact and Legacy

The story of Pandora's Box has had a lasting impact on Western culture. It has been referenced and reinterpreted in various forms of art, literature, and philosophy. The phrase "Pandora's Box" has entered the vernacular as a metaphor for actions that unleash unforeseen and often uncontrollable consequences. This enduring metaphor continues to resonate in discussions about scientific, technological, and ethical issues.

In literature, authors have used the myth to explore themes of innocence, curiosity, and the human condition. The image of Pandora, poised to open the jar, captures a moment of pivotal decision-making that reflects broader questions about human agency and destiny.

Pandora's Dual Legacy

Pandora herself is a complex figure in Greek mythology. On one hand, she is the bringer of suffering, the instrument of divine punishment. On the other hand, she embodies qualities of beauty, intelligence, and resourcefulness. Her dual legacy mirrors the ambivalence with which ancient Greeks viewed the role of women and the inherent complexities of human nature.

Modern Interpretations

In modern times, the myth of Pandora's Box continues to be a source of inspiration and reflection. It raises questions about the ethical implications of curiosity and the pursuit of knowledge. For instance, in the context of scientific advancements, the myth serves as a cautionary tale about the potential risks of unchecked exploration and experimentation.

Additionally, the concept of hope remaining in the jar has been interpreted in various ways. Some view it as a form of consolation, suggesting that even in the face of overwhelming difficulties, hope provides the strength to persevere. Others interpret it as a reminder that hope itself can be elusive and fragile, requiring careful nurturing.

Conclusion

The myth of Pandora's Box is a profound narrative that delves into the origins of human suffering and the enduring presence of hope. It captures the complexity of human nature, the consequences of curiosity, and the interplay between divine will and human action. Through Pandora's story, we are reminded of the intricate balance between knowledge and ignorance, joy and sorrow, and despair and hope.

This myth continues to resonate across cultures and generations, offering timeless lessons about the human experience. It invites us to reflect on our own actions and their potential impacts, urging us to consider the delicate balance between exploring the unknown and respecting the boundaries of the known. In the end, Pandora's Box is not just a story of punishment and suffering, but also a testament to the enduring power of hope and the resilience of the human spirit.

1.6 SUMMARY AND KEY TAKEAWAYS

Summary

In this chapter, we explored the foundational myths of Greek mythology that explain the origins of the gods and the world. We began with the chaotic void from which the first primordial deities emerged, setting the stage for the creation and order of the cosmos. We then delved into the reign of the Titans, a period marked by stability and abundance but also by the ominous prophecy that led to their downfall.

The rise of the Olympian gods, spearheaded by Zeus, highlighted the dramatic conflict and ultimate victory that established a new divine order. Finally, we examined the myth of Prometheus and the creation of man, as well as the story of Pandora's Box, which provides a profound explanation for the presence of evil and suffering in the world, balanced by the enduring presence of hope.

Key Takeaways

Chaos and Creation Myths:

- Greek mythology begins with Chaos, a formless void from which the primordial deities emerged.
- Gaia (Earth) and Uranus (Sky) produced the first generation of Titans.
- Cronus overthrew Uranus, leading to a new era of Titan rule.

The Titans and Their Reign:

- The Titans, led by Cronus, ruled during the Golden Age, a time of peace and prosperity.
- Fearing a prophecy that one of his children would overthrow him, Cronus swallowed his offspring at birth.
- Rhea saved her youngest son, Zeus, who later liberated his siblings and led the Olympians in a war against the Titans.

The Rise of the Olympian Gods:

- o Zeus, after freeing his siblings, led the Olympians in the Titanomachy, a ten-year war against the Titans.
- o With the help of powerful allies like the Cyclopes and the Hecatoncheires, the Olympians defeated the Titans.
- o The Olympians established a new divine order, with Zeus, Poseidon, and Hades ruling the sky, sea, and underworld, respectively.

Prometheus and the Creation of Man:

- o Prometheus created humans from clay and defied Zeus by giving them fire, symbolizing knowledge and civilization.
- o As punishment, Zeus condemned Prometheus to eternal torment and sought to punish humanity through Pandora.
- o Pandora's curiosity led to the release of evils into the world, leaving only hope inside the jar.

The Myth of Pandora's Box:

- o Pandora, created by the gods as a punishment for humanity, opened a jar containing all the evils of the world.
- o The release of these evils marked the end of the Golden Age and the beginning of human suffering.
- o Hope remained in the jar, symbolizing the resilience of the human spirit and the presence of optimism amidst adversity.

Reflective Questions

- How do the themes of creation, rebellion, and order in these myths reflect the ancient Greeks' understanding of the world?
- In what ways do the myths of Prometheus and Pandora explain human suffering and the human condition?
- What lessons can we draw from the stories of the Titans and the Olympians about power, authority, and the cycle of succession?

1.7 MYTHOLOGY QUIZ 1

Test your knowledge about the myths covered in this chapter with the following questions:

1. **What was the primordial void from which the first deities emerged called?**

   A) Gaia

   B) Chaos

   C) Tartarus

   D) Nyx

2. **Who were the parents of the first generation of Titans?**

   A) Zeus and Hera

   B) Cronus and Rhea

   C) Gaia and Uranus

   D) Oceanus and Tethys

3. **What did Cronus do to prevent the prophecy of being overthrown by his children?**

   A) Banished them to Tartarus

   B) Swallowed them at birth

   C) Imprisoned them in a cave

   D) Turned them into stone

4. **Who helped Zeus to free his siblings from Cronus?**

   A) Athena

   B) Prometheus

   C) Metis

   D) Hades

5. **What did Prometheus steal from the gods to give to humanity?**

   A) Knowledge

   B) Immortality

   C) Fire

   D) Water

6. **What was contained in the jar (often referred to as a box) given to Pandora?**

   A) Treasures and gifts

   B) Secrets of the gods

   C) All the evils of the world

   D) Powers of the Titans

7. **What remained in Pandora's jar after she closed it?**

   A) Wisdom

   B) Strength

   C) Hope

   D) Fear

Note: Answers to the quiz can be found in the "Answer Key" section in the Appendix.

CHAPTER 2:
THE TWELVE OLYMPIANS

2.1 ZEUS: KING OF THE GODS

Welcome to the world of the Twelve Olympians, the principal deities in Greek mythology who reside atop Mount Olympus. At the helm of this divine council is Zeus, the King of the Gods. Known for his powerful thunderbolts and unyielding authority, Zeus plays a central role in many myths and legends.

The Birth and Rise of Zeus

Zeus's story begins with a dramatic and dangerous birth. As we've touched on earlier, he was the youngest son of the Titans Cronus and Rhea. Cronus, fearful of a prophecy that foretold his downfall at the hands of one of his children, swallowed each of them at birth. But Rhea, determined to save her youngest, hid Zeus in a cave on Crete and gave Cronus a stone wrapped in swaddling clothes, which he swallowed instead.

Raised in secret, Zeus grew strong and cunning. Once he reached adulthood, he set out to overthrow his father and free his siblings. With the help of Metis, he concocted a potion that forced Cronus to vomit up his brothers and sisters. Together, they waged a ten-year war, known as the Titanomachy, against the Titans. With the support of powerful allies like the Cyclopes and the Hecatoncheires, Zeus and his siblings triumphed, establishing a new order of gods.

Zeus's Dominion and Symbols

As the ruler of the heavens, Zeus's domain included the sky, weather, law, order, and fate. His primary weapon was the thunderbolt, a gift from the Cyclopes, which he wielded with terrifying precision. His symbols include the eagle, the oak tree, and the aegis—a protective cloak often depicted as a shield.

Zeus's authority was unparalleled. He presided over the gods and mortals, enforcing justice and maintaining order in the universe. Despite his omnipotence, Zeus was known for his temper and his susceptibility to emotion, often acting out of jealousy, love, or vengeance.

The Many Loves of Zeus

One of the most famous aspects of Zeus's mythology is his numerous love affairs. Despite being married to Hera, the Queen of the Gods, Zeus had many consorts and children. These relationships often led to conflict and drama, both among the gods and mortals.

Some of his notable liaisons include:

- Leda, whom he seduced in the form of a swan, leading to the birth of Helen of Troy and the Dioscuri twins, Castor andPollux.
- Europa, whom he abducted while disguised as a bull, resulting in the birth of King Minos of Crete.
- Danaë, whom he visited as a golden shower, leading to the birth of Perseus, the hero who would later slay Medusa.

These affairs and their consequences are a recurring theme in Greek mythology, often serving as the foundation for many epic tales and heroic journeys.

Zeus as a God of Justice

Despite his personal flaws, Zeus was revered as a god of justice and moral authority. He upheld the laws of hospitality, known as xenia, and punished those who violated these sacred customs. Tales of his punishments are numerous and often severe, reflecting the importance of maintaining order and respect within society.

One such story is that of Sisyphus, the king who dared to defy Zeus by tricking the gods and escaping death. As punishment, Zeus condemned him to an eternity of rolling a boulder up a hill, only for it to roll back down each time he neared the top. This myth underscores the futility of attempting to outwit the divine order and the relentless nature of divine justice.

Zeus's Role in Human Affairs

Zeus's influence extended beyond the divine realm into the lives of mortals. He was often invoked in oaths and was believed to watch over all human actions, rewarding the virtuous and punishing the wicked. His presence was a constant reminder of the gods' interest and intervention in human affairs.

One of the most famous myths involving Zeus's intervention is the story of the Trojan War. When Paris, a prince of Troy, abducted Helen, the wife of the Spartan king Menelaus, Zeus's will played a significant role in the unfolding events. The gods, under Zeus's direction, took sides in the conflict, influencing battles and the fates of warriors, demonstrating Zeus's omnipresent influence over both gods and men.

Cultural Impact and Legacy

Zeus's legacy is vast and enduring. He has been depicted in countless works of art, literature, and theater throughout the centuries. From the grand statues in ancient Greek temples to modern interpretations in movies and books, Zeus remains a symbol of power, authority, and the complexities of divine rule.

In ancient Greece, his worship was central to many religious practices. Major festivals like the Olympic Games, held in his honor, celebrated athletic prowess and religious devotion. Temples dedicated to Zeus, such as the grand temple at Olympia, were architectural marvels that drew worshippers from across the Greek world.

Conclusion

Zeus, as the King of the Gods, embodies the grandeur and complexity of Greek mythology. His stories of love, justice, and power offer a window into the ancient Greek understanding of the divine and its relationship with the mortal world. Through his mythos, we gain insight into themes of authority, morality, and the human condition.

By understanding Zeus's character and his impact on Greek mythology, we can better appreciate the rich tapestry of stories that continue to influence Western culture and thought. As we delve deeper into the lives of the other Olympians, Zeus's presence as a central figure will remain a guiding force, reflecting the intricate interplay of power, justice, and human emotion in the mythological cosmos.

2.2 HERA: QUEEN OF THE GODS

Hera, the Queen of the Gods, is one of the most prominent and complex figures in Greek mythology. As the wife of Zeus and the goddess of marriage, women, childbirth, and family, Hera's influence extends across both the divine and mortal realms. Her stories reflect her powerful position, fierce loyalty, and sometimes tumultuous relationship with Zeus.

Hera's Origins and Marriage to Zeus

Hera was the daughter of the Titans Cronus and Rhea, making her a sister to Zeus, Poseidon, Hades, Demeter, and Hestia. Like her siblings, Hera was swallowed by Cronus at birth and later rescued by Zeus. Hera's marriage to Zeus was both a symbol of unity and a source of endless drama.

Despite their tumultuous relationship, Hera's marriage to Zeus solidified her status as the Queen of the Gods. Their union was not merely a personal relationship but also a political alliance, representing the integration of their respective domains and powers. This dynamic partnership, filled with both love and conflict, played a central role in many myths.

Hera's Role and Symbols

Hera's primary domain was marriage and the sanctity of the family. She was revered as the protector of married women and presided over all aspects of marriage and childbirth. Her symbols include the peacock, with its beautiful and all-seeing eyes, representing her watchfulness and regal nature. The cow, another of her symbols, signifies her nurturing aspects and her connection to fertility.

As the goddess of marriage, Hera was often depicted as a matronly figure, wearing a crown and holding a scepter or a pomegranate, symbolizing fertility and plenty. Her presence was a constant reminder of the sacredness and responsibilities of marital vows.

Hera's Jealousy and Vengeance

Hera is perhaps most famously known for her fierce jealousy and her relentless vengeance against Zeus's numerous lovers and their offspring. Her actions, while often harsh, were driven by a deep sense of loyalty and a desire to uphold the sanctity of marriage. This aspect of her character reveals the complexities of her role as both a loving wife and a powerful goddess.

One of the most famous stories involving Hera's jealousy is her persecution of **Heracles (Hercules)**, the son of Zeus and the mortal woman Alcmene. From the moment of his birth, Hera sought to make Heracles's life difficult. She sent snakes to kill him in his cradle, but the infant Heracles, displaying his future strength, strangled them. Later, Hera drove Heracles mad, causing him to kill his own children, which set the stage for his Twelve Labors, a series of nearly impossible tasks meant to atone for his sins.

Another example is the story of **Io**, a priestess of Hera who caught Zeus's eye. To hide Io from Hera's wrath, Zeus transformed her into a white heifer. However, Hera saw through the disguise and sent a gadfly to torment Io, driving her to wander the earth endlessly. This relentless pursuit illustrates Hera's determination to punish those involved in her husband's infidelities.

Hera's Compassion and Protection

Despite her reputation for jealousy, Hera also displayed compassion and a protective nature, particularly towards women and children. She was often invoked in prayers and rituals related to marriage and childbirth, and many looked to her for protection and guidance.

One notable myth that highlights Hera's protective side is the story of **Jason and the Argonauts**. When Jason set out on his quest for the Golden Fleece, Hera supported him because he had once helped her when she was disguised as an old woman. She provided guidance and aid throughout his journey, showing her favor and protection to those who honored her.

Hera's Influence on Mortal Affairs

Hera's involvement in mortal affairs extended beyond her relationships with Zeus's lovers and their children. She often played a significant role in major events and conflicts, demonstrating her far-reaching influence. During the Trojan War, Hera was a fierce advocate for the Greeks, driven by her hatred for Paris, the Trojan prince who had judged Aphrodite to be more beautiful than her.

In the famous **Judgment of Paris**, Hera offered Paris power and kingship if he chose her as the fairest. When he instead chose Aphrodite, who promised him the love of Helen of Sparta, Hera's anger towards Troy was ignited. Throughout the war, she worked tirelessly to aid the Greek heroes and thwart the Trojans, showcasing her strategic mind and determination.

Cultural Impact and Worship

Hera's worship was widespread in ancient Greece, with numerous temples and festivals dedicated to her. The Heraia, a festival held in her honor, included athletic competitions for women, reflecting her role as a protector of women and marriage. The Temple of Hera in Olympia and the Heraion of Samos are two of the most significant sanctuaries dedicated to her, highlighting her importance in Greek religion.

In art and literature, Hera was often depicted as a majestic and imposing figure, embodying the ideals of womanhood and marital fidelity. Her stories, while sometimes casting her in a negative light, also reveal her strength, resilience, and dedication to her role as the Queen of the Gods.

Conclusion

Hera, as the Queen of the Gods, is a multifaceted deity whose stories reflect the complexities of her character and her significant influence in Greek mythology. Her fierce loyalty, combined with her protective nature, paints a picture of a goddess who embodies the sanctity of marriage and the power of divine authority.

Through her myths, we gain insight into the ancient Greek values surrounding marriage, fidelity, and the roles of women. Hera's legacy endures as a testament to the enduring power and influence of the divine feminine in mythology and culture. Her tales, filled with both conflict and compassion, continue to captivate and inspire, offering timeless lessons about loyalty, justice, and the human condition.

2.3 POSEIDON: GOD OF THE SEA

Poseidon, one of the Twelve Olympians, is the mighty god of the sea, earthquakes, and horses. Known for his powerful trident and tempestuous nature, Poseidon plays a crucial role in Greek mythology. His influence extends across the vast oceans and deep into the earth, making him one of the most revered and feared deities.

Poseidon's Origins and Symbols

Poseidon was the son of the Titans Cronus and Rhea, making him a brother to Zeus, Hades, Hera, Demeter, and Hestia. Like his siblings, Poseidon was swallowed at birth by Cronus and later freed by Zeus. After the defeat of the Titans, the three brothers—Zeus, Poseidon, and Hades—drew lots to divide the realms of the universe. Poseidon claimed the sea, becoming its undisputed ruler.

Poseidon's primary symbol is the trident, a three-pronged spear forged by the Cyclopes. With this powerful weapon, Poseidon could stir the seas, create storms, and cause earthquakes, earning him the epithet "Earth-shaker." His other symbols include the horse and the dolphin. The horse, in particular, is significant as Poseidon was believed to have created the first horse and was often depicted riding a chariot drawn by magnificent steeds.

Poseidon's Realm and Powers

As the god of the sea, Poseidon's domain encompassed all bodies of water, from the vast oceans to rivers and springs. Mariners and fishermen revered him, seeking his favor for safe voyages and bountiful catches. However, Poseidon's temperament was notoriously unpredictable, reflecting the capricious nature of the sea itself. He could be both generous and vengeful, calm and stormy.

Poseidon's powers were not limited to the sea. He also had dominion over earthquakes, a force that symbolized his ability to shake the very foundations of the earth. This dual control over water and land made him a deity of immense power and influence, capable of altering the natural world with a single stroke of his trident.

Poseidon's Relationships and Offspring

Poseidon was known for his numerous romantic entanglements, much like his brother Zeus. He married Amphitrite, a sea nymph and one of the fifty Nereids, who became the queen of the sea. Together, they had several children, including Triton, a merman who served as his father's herald.

Poseidon's love affairs were not confined to the sea. He pursued many mortal women and goddesses, resulting in a multitude of offspring. Some of his notable children include:

- **Theseus**, the hero who defeated the Minotaur and became the king of Athens, was often regarded as Poseidon's son.
- **Polyphemus**, the Cyclops encountered by Odysseus in Homer's "Odyssey," was a son of Poseidon and the sea nymph Thoosa.
- **Pegasus**, the winged horse, sprang from the blood of Medusa when she was beheaded by Perseus. Poseidon was Medusa's lover before her transformation into a Gorgon.

Poseidon's progeny often inherited his strength and volatile nature, contributing to many legendary tales and heroic feats in Greek mythology.

Poseidon's Conflicts and Feuds

Poseidon's temper and pride frequently led him into conflicts with other gods and mortals. One of his most famous disputes was with Athena over the patronage of Athens. Both gods desired to be the city's protector, and the competition was fierce. Poseidon struck the Acropolis with his trident, creating a saltwater spring, while Athena offered the olive tree, symbolizing peace and prosperity. The Athenians chose Athena's gift, and Poseidon, though angered, accepted the decision.

Another notable conflict involved the Trojan War. Poseidon harbored a deep grudge against the Trojans because King Laomedon had refused to pay him for building the walls of Troy. During the war, Poseidon sided with the Greeks, using his powers to aid them in battle. However, his support for the Greeks was also marked by personal vendettas and shifting loyalties, illustrating his unpredictable nature.

Poseidon's Wrath

Poseidon's wrath could be terrifying and far-reaching. His anger towards Odysseus, as depicted in the "Odyssey," is a prime example. After Odysseus blinded Polyphemus, Poseidon cursed him, condemning him to wander the seas for ten years before returning home. This epic journey, filled with trials and tribulations, showcases Poseidon's relentless pursuit of vengeance and the formidable obstacles he could place in the path of those who wronged him.

Cultural Impact and Worship

Poseidon was widely worshiped throughout ancient Greece, particularly in coastal cities and islands where the sea was integral to daily life. Temples dedicated to Poseidon, such as the famous Temple of Poseidon at Sounion, were important religious sites where sailors and fishermen would offer sacrifices to gain his favor.

Festivals like the Isthmian Games, held near Corinth, honored Poseidon with athletic competitions and sacrifices. These games were one of the major Panhellenic festivals, reflecting Poseidon's significant cultural and religious influence.

In art and literature, Poseidon was often depicted as a robust, bearded god holding his trident, either standing majestically or riding his chariot over the waves. His image conveyed both his dominion over the sea and his formidable power as one of the most influential Olympian gods.

Conclusion

Poseidon, the god of the sea, earthquakes, and horses, is a figure of immense power and complexity in Greek mythology. His stories are filled with acts of creation and destruction, love and vengeance, reflecting the dual nature of the sea itself. As a central deity in the Greek pantheon, Poseidon's influence extended across both the divine and mortal realms, shaping the world with his mighty trident.

Through Poseidon's myths, we gain insight into the ancient Greeks' relationship with the natural world, particularly the sea, which was both a source of sustenance and a force of unpredictability. His legacy endures in the rich tapestry of Greek mythology, reminding us of the power and majesty of the ancient gods.

2.4 DEMETER: GODDESS OF THE HARVEST

Demeter, the goddess of the harvest, agriculture, and fertility, is one of the Twelve Olympians whose influence is deeply rooted in the cycles of nature and human sustenance. Her stories are closely linked to the changing seasons and the eternal connection between life and death, reflecting the ancient Greeks' reverence for the earth and its bounty.

Demeter's Origins and Symbols

Demeter was the daughter of the Titans Cronus and Rhea, making her a sister to Zeus, Poseidon, Hades, Hera, and Hestia. Like her siblings, she was swallowed by Cronus at birth and later freed by Zeus. Demeter's realm encompassed all aspects of agriculture, from the sowing of seeds to the harvest, making her one of the most vital deities for ancient Greek society, which depended heavily on farming.

Her symbols include the cornucopia, a horn of plenty that represents abundance and nourishment; sheaves of wheat, symbolizing the harvest; and the poppy, a flower often associated with fertility. Demeter is typically depicted holding a torch, symbolizing her search for her daughter, Persephone, or carrying sheaves of wheat, reflecting her role as the provider of the earth's bounty.

The Abduction of Persephone

One of the most significant myths involving Demeter is the abduction of her daughter, Persephone, by Hades, the god of the underworld. This story not only explains the origin of the seasons but also illustrates Demeter's deep maternal love and the profound impact of her grief on the world.

Persephone, the daughter of Demeter and Zeus, was a beautiful maiden who caught the eye of Hades. One day, while she was gathering flowers, the ground opened up, and Hades emerged, capturing Persephone and taking her to the underworld to be his queen. Demeter, unaware of her daughter's fate, began a frantic search that lasted for days. She roamed the earth with a torch, refusing to rest until she found Persephone.

During her search, Demeter neglected her duties as the goddess of the harvest, and the earth became barren. Crops failed, and famine spread, causing immense suffering among mortals. Realizing that the survival of humanity was at stake, Zeus intervened. He sent Hermes, the messenger god, to the underworld to negotiate Persephone's release.

Hades agreed to let Persephone go, but before she left, he tricked her into eating a few seeds of a pomegranate. Because she had eaten the food of the underworld, Persephone was bound to return there for a part of each year. A compromise was reached: Persephone would spend two-thirds of the year with Demeter on earth and one-third of the year with Hades in the underworld.

The Eleusinian Mysteries

The myth of Demeter and Persephone was central to the Eleusinian Mysteries, one of the most important religious rites in ancient Greece. These mysteries, held in Eleusis near Athens, were secretive ceremonies that promised to initiate knowledge of the afterlife and a closer relationship with the gods. Participants underwent a series of rituals, including fasting, purification, and dramatic reenactments of the myth, culminating in a mystical revelation.

The Eleusinian Mysteries emphasized themes of life, death, and rebirth, reflecting the agricultural cycle of planting, growth, harvest, and dormancy. By participating in these rites, initiates sought to gain favor from Demeter and Persephone and to ensure a bountiful harvest and personal spiritual renewal.

Demeter's Influence and Worship

Demeter's influence was far-reaching, encompassing not only the physical nourishment of humanity but also the spiritual and emotional aspects of life. As the provider of the harvest, she was essential for the survival and prosperity of ancient Greek communities. Her festivals, such as the Thesmophoria and the Eleusinian Mysteries, were major events that celebrated fertility, agriculture, and the mysteries of life and death.

The Thesmophoria was an agricultural festival held in honor of Demeter and Persephone, celebrated primarily by women. It involved rituals that promoted fertility and the well-being of the community. Participants would plant seeds, offer sacrifices, and engage in various rites to honor the goddesses and ensure a successful harvest.

Demeter's temples were often located in rural areas, where her presence was most keenly felt. The Temple of Demeter at Eleusis, where the Eleusinian Mysteries were held, was one of the most significant religious sites in ancient Greece. Here, worshippers would gather to honor the goddess, participate in rituals, and seek her blessings for abundant crops and fertility.

Demeter's Relationships and Offspring

Demeter's relationships with other gods and mortals further illustrate her nurturing and sometimes protective nature. Besides Persephone, she had several other children, each with their own stories and significance:

- **Plutus**, the god of wealth, was born from Demeter's union with Iasion, a mortal. Plutus symbolized the wealth and abundance that came from the earth.
- **Despoina** and **Arion**, both born from her union with Poseidon, each had roles in various myths, though they were less prominent than Persephone.

59

Demeter's interactions with mortals also highlight her benevolence and protective instincts. One such story involves **Triptolemus**, a prince of Eleusis, whom Demeter taught the secrets of agriculture. She gave him a chariot drawn by winged dragons and sent him across the world to teach humanity how to cultivate crops, spreading the knowledge of agriculture far and wide.

Cultural Impact and Legacy

Demeter's legacy is deeply embedded in the fabric of Greek culture and mythology. As the goddess of the harvest, she represents the vital connection between humanity and the earth. Her myths convey themes of motherhood, loss, and renewal, reflecting the cyclical nature of life and the dependence of human societies on the natural world.

n art and literature, Demeter is often depicted as a matronly figure, embodying the nurturing aspects of motherhood and the life-giving force of nature. Her stories, particularly the abduction of Persephone, have inspired countless works of art, from ancient vase paintings to modern interpretations in literature and theater. For instance, in the Homeric Hymn to Demeter, the abduction of Persephone and Demeter's subsequent grief are poignantly described, emphasizing the powerful bond between mother and daughter. This myth has also influenced numerous modern literary works, such as the play "Persephone" by Mary Zimmerman and various retellings in contemporary novels. Artists, too, have been inspired by this myth, with works like Frederic Leighton's painting "The Return of Persephone," capturing the dramatic reunion between mother and daughter. These examples illustrate how the myth of Demeter and Persephone continues to resonate through the ages, highlighting its profound impact on cultural and artistic expressions.

Conclusion

Demeter, the goddess of the harvest, stands as a powerful and nurturing figure in Greek mythology. Her stories of love, loss, and renewal offer profound insights into the ancient Greeks' relationship with the earth and the cycles of nature. Through her myths, we understand the significance of agriculture and fertility, and the deep emotional bonds between mothers and their children.

By honoring Demeter, the ancient Greeks acknowledged their dependence on the earth's bounty and the importance of maintaining harmony with the natural world. Her legacy continues to resonate, reminding us of the enduring connection between humanity and the land that sustains us.

2.5 ATHENA: GODDESS OF WISDOM

Athena, the goddess of wisdom, war, and crafts, is one of the most revered deities in Greek mythology. Known for her strategic skill in warfare and her patronage of arts and sciences, Athena embodies the combination of intellect and strength. Her birth and her role in various myths highlight her importance in both divine and mortal realms.

The Birth of Athena

Athena's birth is one of the most extraordinary tales in Greek mythology. According to myth, she sprang fully grown and armored from the forehead of Zeus. This unusual birth was the result of a prophecy that the child Metis, the goddess of wisdom and Zeus's first wife, was carrying would surpass him. To prevent this, Zeus swallowed Metis while she was pregnant. However, the child continued to grow inside Zeus, and one day he experienced a terrible headache. Hephaestus, the god of blacksmiths, struck Zeus's head with an axe, and out sprang Athena, fully formed and ready for battle.

This dramatic entrance symbolized Athena's unique qualities: she was born of her father's head, representing intellect and wisdom, and she emerged in full armor, signifying her warrior nature. Unlike many other gods and goddesses, Athena was always depicted as a virgin deity, embodying purity and rationality.

Athena's Symbols and Attributes

Athena's symbols include the owl, representing wisdom and watchfulness, and the olive tree, symbolizing peace and prosperity. The aegis, a protective cloak often depicted as a shield with the head of the Gorgon Medusa, is another key attribute. This powerful symbol of protection was a gift from Zeus and was said to strike fear into her enemies.

Athena is frequently depicted wearing a helmet and carrying a shield and spear, underscoring her role as a warrior goddess. Her appearance often reflects her dual aspects of war and wisdom—both a fierce protector and a guide for those who seek knowledge.

Athena as a Warrior Goddess

Athena's role as a goddess of war is distinct from that of Ares, the god of war. While Ares represents the chaotic and brutal aspects of warfare, Athena embodies strategic warfare and defense. She is the goddess of disciplined and rational combat, favoring tactics and planning over sheer force.

One of the most notable examples of Athena's martial prowess is her assistance to heroes such as Odysseus and Perseus. In Homer's "Odyssey," Athena is a constant guide and protector of Odysseus, helping him navigate the many challenges he faces on his journey home from the Trojan War. Her wisdom and strategic thinking are crucial in ensuring his survival and eventual success.

In the myth of Perseus, Athena provides the hero with the mirrored shield he uses to defeat Medusa, allowing him to view her reflection rather than looking directly at her and being turned to stone. This act of guidance and provision of tools necessary for victory highlights Athena's role as a mentor and protector of heroes.

Athena as a Patron of the Arts and Crafts

Beyond her martial aspects, Athena is also the patron goddess of arts and crafts, particularly weaving. Her association with weaving is celebrated in the myth of Arachne, a talented mortal weaver who challenged Athena to a weaving contest. Although Arachne's skills were exceptional, her hubris in comparing herself to a goddess led to her downfall. Athena transformed her into a spider, condemning her to weave for eternity. This story underscores the importance of humility and the consequences of pride.

Athena's patronage extended to various other crafts and intellectual pursuits. She was seen as a guiding force behind all forms of wisdom, from practical skills like weaving and metalwork to strategic and philosophical thought. Her influence was evident in the everyday lives of the Greeks, who looked to her for inspiration and guidance in their work.

The Founding of Athens

One of the most significant myths involving Athena is the founding of Athens. The city was named after her following a contest with Poseidon over its patronage. Poseidon struck the Acropolis with his trident, creating a saltwater spring, while Athena offered the olive tree, symbolizing peace and prosperity. The citizens of Athens chose Athena's gift, and the city was named in her honor. The olive tree became a central symbol of the city, representing its wealth and agricultural success.

The Parthenon, a magnificent temple on the Acropolis, was dedicated to Athena and stood as a testament to her importance in Athenian society. The temple housed a colossal statue of Athena Parthenos, crafted by the sculptor Phidias, symbolizing her protective and guiding presence over the city.

Athena's Role in Human Affairs

Athena was deeply involved in the affairs of mortals, guiding and protecting those who demonstrated intelligence, bravery, and justice. Her relationship with heroes like Odysseus, Heracles, and Perseus reflects her role as a mentor and protector. She provided them with the wisdom and tools they needed to overcome their challenges, embodying the principle that success comes from a combination of intellect and strength.

Her interventions were not limited to grand heroics but also extended to the everyday lives of the Greeks. Athena was invoked for guidance in various aspects of life, from military strategy to domestic crafts. Her presence was a constant reminder of the value of wisdom and the importance of balance between intellect and action.

Cultural Impact and Worship

Athena was widely worshiped across Greece, with numerous temples and festivals dedicated to her. The Panathenaic Festival, held annually in Athens, was one of the most important religious celebrations, featuring athletic and artistic competitions, sacrifices, and a grand procession to the Acropolis. The festival celebrated Athena's birthday and honored her contributions to the city.

In literature and art, Athena was depicted as a powerful and wise figure, embodying the ideals of the Greek city-state. Her stories and images conveyed values of wisdom, courage, and justice, influencing Greek culture and philosophy profoundly.

Conclusion

Athena, the goddess of wisdom, war, and crafts, stands as a symbol of intellect and strength in Greek mythology. Her myths reveal a goddess who values strategic thinking and practical skills, guiding and protecting both heroes and ordinary people. Through her stories, we see the ancient Greek appreciation for wisdom, the arts, and disciplined combat.

As we delve into the lives of the other Olympians, Athena's legacy as a wise and powerful deity continues to inspire and teach us about the importance of balance between intellect and action, and the enduring power of knowledge and skill.

2.6 APOLLO: GOD OF THE SUN

Apollo, the god of the sun, music, prophecy, healing, and the arts, is one of the most multifaceted and revered deities in Greek mythology. His influence extends across various domains, making him a central figure in many myths and an embodiment of harmony and enlightenment.

Apollo's Origins and Symbols

Apollo is the son of Zeus and Leto and the twin brother of Artemis, the goddess of the hunt. His birth was fraught with difficulty, as Hera, in her jealousy, forbade Leto from giving birth on solid ground. Leto finally found refuge on the floating island of Delos, where she gave birth to Apollo and Artemis.

Apollo is often depicted as a handsome, beardless youth with long hair, embodying the ideal of youthful beauty and vitality. His primary symbols include the lyre, representing his mastery of music and the arts; the laurel wreath, a symbol of victory and honor; and the bow and arrow, signifying his prowess in archery. The sun itself, symbolizing light, truth, and knowledge, is perhaps his most iconic attribute.

Apollo as the Sun God

Although Apollo is commonly associated with the sun, it is important to note that the actual personification of the sun was the Titan Helios. However, over time, Apollo became increasingly linked with the sun and its life-giving qualities. He was seen as a bringer of light and clarity, dispelling darkness and ignorance. This association with the sun underscored his role as a god of prophecy and enlightenment.

Apollo's daily journey across the sky in his chariot, pulling the sun from east to west, symbolizes his essential role in the natural order. This journey also represents the spread of knowledge and truth, illuminating the world both literally and figuratively.

Apollo and the Oracle of Delphi

One of Apollo's most significant roles was as the god of prophecy and oracles. The Oracle of Delphi, located on the slopes of Mount Parnassus, was the most famous and revered oracle in ancient Greece. It was believed that Apollo spoke through Pythia, the priestess of the oracle, who delivered cryptic prophecies to those seeking guidance.

The story of how Apollo came to be associated with Delphi begins with his defeat of the Python, a serpent that guarded the site. After slaying the Python, Apollo claimed Delphi as his own and established the oracle. This act of conquering the serpent, a symbol of chaos and earthbound power, highlighted Apollo's role as a bringer of order and divine insight.

People from all over Greece and beyond would travel to Delphi to seek Apollo's wisdom on matters ranging from personal decisions to state affairs. The Delphic Oracle played a crucial role in Greek society, influencing politics, religion, and daily life through its pronouncements.

Apollo's Musical Talents

Apollo was also the god of music, poetry, and the arts, often depicted with his lyre, an instrument given to him by Hermes. He was considered the leader of the Muses, the goddesses of inspiration in literature, science, and the arts. Under Apollo's guidance, the Muses inspired creativity and knowledge, fostering the cultural achievements of ancient Greece.

One of Apollo's notable musical myths involves a contest with Marsyas, a satyr who challenged Apollo to a musical duel. Marsyas played the aulos, a double-reeded instrument, while Apollo played the lyre. Despite Marsyas's skill, Apollo won the contest by playing his lyre upside down and demanding that Marsyas do the same, which he could not. As punishment for his hubris, Marsyas was flayed alive, a stark reminder of the consequences of challenging a god.

Apollo's Healing Abilities

Apollo was also revered as a god of healing and medicine. He was the father of Asclepius, the god of medicine, whom he conceived with the mortal woman Coronis. Asclepius inherited Apollo's healing abilities and became a central figure in ancient Greek medicine, with sanctuaries dedicated to him where people would go to seek cures for their ailments.

Apollo's role as a healer is further illustrated in his association with the plague. He could both bring and avert plagues, reflecting his dual nature as a god who could cause destruction but also provide relief and healing. This aspect of Apollo's character underscored the balance between life and death, health and sickness.

Apollo's Romantic Affairs

Apollo's romantic life was as complex as his many roles. He had numerous love affairs, both with mortals and other deities. One of the most tragic stories is that of Daphne, a nymph who caught Apollo's eye. When she rejected his advances, she prayed to her father, the river god Peneus, for help. To escape Apollo, Daphne was transformed into a laurel tree. Stricken with grief, Apollo declared the laurel tree sacred and wore a crown of its leaves to honor her.

Another significant love story involves Hyacinthus, a handsome Spartan youth whom Apollo loved deeply. They often practiced throwing the discus together. One day, a discus thrown by Apollo was deflected by the jealous god Zephyrus, striking Hyacinthus in the head and killing him. From Hyacinthus's blood, Apollo caused a beautiful flower, the hyacinth, to bloom in his memory.

Apollo's Influence and Worship

Apollo was worshiped widely across the Greek world, with many temples and festivals dedicated to him. The Pythian Games, held every four years at Delphi, were among the most important religious festivals, featuring athletic and musical competitions in Apollo's honor. These games celebrated his victory over the Python and his role as a god of music and prophecy.

Temples dedicated to Apollo were architectural masterpieces, often featuring grand columns and intricate sculptures. The Temple of Apollo at Delphi, one of the most famous, housed the Delphic Oracle and attracted pilgrims from all over the ancient world. Other significant temples include those at Delos, Didyma, and Claros.

Conclusion

Apollo, the god of the sun, music, prophecy, and healing, is a deity of remarkable versatility and influence in Greek mythology. His myths reveal a god who embodies the ideals of beauty, wisdom, and enlightenment, guiding mortals and gods alike with his radiant presence. Through his various domains, Apollo represents the harmony of the cosmos, the pursuit of knowledge, and the balance between light and darkness.

As we continue to explore the lives of the other Olympians, Apollo's legacy as a multifaceted god will remain a testament to the richness and complexity of Greek mythology. His stories remind us of the power of art, the importance of wisdom, and the enduring quest for understanding in our world.

2.7 ARTEMIS: GODDESS OF THE HUNT

Artemis, the goddess of the hunt, wilderness, and childbirth, is one of the most fascinating and revered figures in Greek mythology. Known for her fierce independence, unwavering chastity, and mastery of the natural world, Artemis embodies the spirit of the untamed wilderness and the protective instincts of a guardian.

Artemis's Origins and Symbols

Artemis is the daughter of Zeus and Leto, and the twin sister of Apollo. Her birth was surrounded by hardship due to Hera's jealousy, but Leto found refuge on the island of Delos, where she gave birth to Artemis and Apollo. Artemis, born first, then assisted her mother in the delivery of her brother, which is why she became associated with childbirth.

Artemis's symbols include the bow and arrow, representing her prowess as a huntress; the deer, symbolizing her connection to the wilderness; and the cypress tree, which is often associated with mourning and immortality. She is frequently depicted with a crescent moon on her forehead, reflecting her role as a lunar goddess and her connection to nighttime and the wilderness.

Artemis as the Huntress

As the goddess of the hunt, Artemis is often portrayed as a young, vigorous woman who roams the forests with her bow and arrows, accompanied by a band of nymphs. She is a skilled hunter, protector of wildlife, and guardian of young women. Her hunting skills are unmatched, and she is both revered and feared for her ability to strike with precision and deadly accuracy.

Artemis's dedication to hunting and her close relationship with nature underscore her role as a protector of the wild. She ensures the balance of nature, sometimes aiding hunters and at other times punishing those who disrespect the natural world. One famous myth involves Actaeon, a mortal hunter who stumbled upon Artemis bathing. In her anger, she transformed him into a stag, and he was subsequently torn apart by his own hunting dogs. This story highlights her fierce protection of her privacy and her domain.

Artemis's Chastity and Independence

One of the most defining aspects of Artemis's character is her commitment to chastity and independence. She vowed to remain a virgin forever, rejecting the advances of both gods and mortals. This vow symbolizes her autonomy and her rejection of the conventional roles expected of women in ancient Greek society.

Artemis's nymph companions were also expected to maintain their chastity. When one of her followers, Callisto, was seduced by Zeus and became pregnant, Artemis transformed her into a bear as punishment. This act underscores the strictness with which Artemis enforced her principles and the high standards she set for herself and her followers.

Artemis as a Protector of Women and Children

Artemis's protective nature extends beyond the wilderness to include women and children, particularly during childbirth. Despite her association with virginity, she was revered as a goddess of childbirth and a protector of women in labor. This duality reflects the ancient Greeks' understanding of the interconnectedness of life and the natural cycles.

One myth that illustrates this aspect of Artemis's character is the story of **Niobe**, who boasted about having more children than Leto, Artemis and Apollo's mother. Offended by this arrogance, Artemis and Apollo killed Niobe's children as a punishment. Although this story is tragic, it highlights the divine protection afforded to those who honor the gods and the consequences of hubris.

Artemis and the Moon

Artemis is also associated with the moon, often depicted as the goddess of the moonlight. This lunar connection links her to the cycles of nature and the mysterious, nocturnal world. The moon's phases symbolize the cyclical nature of life, death, and rebirth, aligning with Artemis's roles in hunting, wilderness, and childbirth.

In this lunar aspect, Artemis complements her brother Apollo, who is associated with the sun. Together, they represent the balance between day and night, light and darkness, rationality and mystery. This duality enhances their significance in Greek mythology, embodying the harmony of opposites.

Artemis's Influence and Worship

Artemis was widely worshiped across ancient Greece, with numerous temples and sanctuaries dedicated to her. One of the most famous was the Temple of Artemis at Ephesus, one of the Seven Wonders of the Ancient World. This grand temple reflected the goddess's importance and the devotion of her followers.

Festivals dedicated to Artemis included the **Brauronia**, celebrated at Brauron, where young girls participated in rituals and dances in honor of the goddess. These rites often involved symbolic acts of hunting and offerings to Artemis, reinforcing her role as a protector and mentor to young women.

Cultural Impact and Legacy

Artemis's legacy extends beyond mythology into the cultural and social practices of ancient Greece. Her stories and worship reflect the values and beliefs of the society, emphasizing the importance of nature, the protection of the vulnerable, and the power of female independence.

In art and literature, Artemis is depicted as a strong, youthful huntress, often accompanied by her nymphs and surrounded by the wilderness. Her image has inspired countless works, from ancient sculptures and vase paintings to modern interpretations in literature and film. One example of her modern portrayal in film is the character of Artemis in the movie "Wonder Woman" (2017), where she appears as one of the Amazon warriors, showcasing her strength and association with nature and the hunt.

Conclusion

Artemis, the goddess of the hunt, wilderness, and childbirth, embodies the spirit of independence, protection, and the natural world in Greek mythology. Her fierce dedication to her principles, combined with her nurturing role as a protector of women and children, makes her a complex and compelling figure. Through her myths, we gain insight into the ancient Greeks' relationship with nature, their reverence for the cycles of life, and the power of female autonomy.

As we continue to explore the lives of the other Olympians, Artemis's legacy as a powerful and independent goddess remains a testament to the richness and depth of Greek mythology. Her stories remind us of the importance of respecting the natural world, the strength found in independence, and the enduring connection between humanity and nature.

2.8 ARES: GOD OF WAR

Ares, the god of war, represents the brutal and violent aspects of conflict in Greek mythology. Unlike Athena, who embodies strategic warfare and wisdom, Ares personifies the chaotic, bloodthirsty nature of battle. His presence on the battlefield is both feared and revered, highlighting the dual nature of war as a force of destruction and a test of strength.

Ares's Origins and Symbols

Ares is the son of Zeus and Hera, making him one of the Olympian gods. Despite his divine parentage, Ares often found himself at odds with other gods, including his father, Zeus, who frequently expressed disdain for Ares's aggressive and reckless nature.

Ares's symbols include the spear and helmet, representing his role as a warrior; the vulture, a bird that follows battlefields and feasts on the dead; and the dog, an animal often associated with the carnage of war. In art, Ares is typically depicted as a muscular, armed warrior, ready for combat.

Ares's Role in Mythology

Ares's role in Greek mythology is predominantly tied to war and conflict. He revels in the chaos and bloodshed of battle, often accompanied by his retinue of deities and personifications associated with war, including Deimos (Terror), Phobos (Fear), and Eris (Strife). These companions emphasize the fearsome and destructive nature of war that Ares embodies.

One of the key myths involving Ares is his affair with Aphrodite, the goddess of love. Despite Aphrodite being married to Hephaestus, the god of blacksmiths, she and Ares engaged in a passionate affair. This relationship produced several children, including Eros (Cupid), the god of love; Anteros, the god of requited love; and Harmonia, the goddess of harmony. The affair between Ares and Aphrodite highlights the contrasting yet intertwined aspects of love and war.

Ares in the Trojan War

Ares played a significant role in the Trojan War, siding with the Trojans against the Greeks. His presence on the battlefield brought fear and destruction, as he fought alongside the Trojan warriors. However, his involvement often led to conflicts with other gods who supported the Greeks, such as Athena and Hera.

During one notable encounter in the war, Ares faced Athena in battle. Athena, representing strategic warfare, easily overpowered Ares, reflecting the Greek belief in the superiority of wisdom and strategy over brute force. This defeat was not an isolated incident; Ares frequently suffered humiliation and setbacks in myths, highlighting his impulsive and reckless nature.

Ares's Relationships and Offspring

Beyond his affair with Aphrodite, Ares had numerous romantic liaisons, resulting in a variety of offspring. Some of his notable children include:

- **Hippolyta**, the Amazonian queen, renowned for her strength and leadership.
- **Cycnus**, a warrior who challenged Heracles and was ultimately slain by him.
- **Diomedes**, a Thracian king known for his man-eating horses, whom Heracles also defeated.

These offspring often inherited Ares's martial prowess and fierce nature, contributing to their own legends and reinforcing Ares's influence in various heroic tales.

Ares's Conflicts and Humiliations

Ares's aggressive temperament frequently led to conflicts with other gods and mortals. His impulsiveness and love of violence often resulted in humiliations, as seen in several myths. One such story involves Ares's capture by the Aloadae, two giant brothers who sought to overthrow the Olympian gods. They trapped Ares in a bronze jar for over a year, showcasing the god's vulnerability and the consequences of his recklessness.

Another significant myth highlights Ares's clash with Hephaestus. After discovering Ares's affair with Aphrodite, Hephaestus crafted a fine net and trapped the lovers in a compromising position, exposing their infidelity to the other gods. This public humiliation underscored Ares's flawed nature and his contentious relationships with the other deities.

Ares's Worship and Cultural Impact

Despite his negative traits and frequent humiliations, Ares was still worshiped in various parts of ancient Greece, though not as widely or enthusiastically as other Olympian gods. His primary cult centers were located in Thrace, a region known for its fierce warriors, and in Sparta, where the militaristic society revered Ares as a symbol of strength and bravery.

In Sparta, Ares was honored with sacrifices and rituals meant to invoke his favor and ensure success in battle. The Spartans, known for their martial prowess, saw Ares as a divine patron who embodied the warrior spirit they valued so highly.

In art and literature, Ares is often depicted as a fearsome and powerful figure, embodying the raw, untamed force of war. His stories serve as cautionary tales about the dangers of unchecked aggression and the importance of strategic thinking in conflict.

Conclusion

Ares, the god of war, represents the destructive and chaotic nature of battle in Greek mythology. His fierce and aggressive personality sets him apart from other deities, reflecting the dual nature of war as both a necessary force and a source of immense suffering. Through his myths, we see the complexities of conflict, the consequences of recklessness, and the intricate relationship between love and war.

As we continue to explore the lives of the other Olympians, Ares's legacy as a symbol of war and aggression remains a testament to the multifaceted nature of the gods in Greek mythology. His stories remind us of the power and peril of conflict, the importance of strategy and wisdom, and the enduring struggle between order and chaos in the world.

2.9 APHRODITE: GODDESS OF LOVE

Aphrodite, the goddess of love, beauty, and desire, is one of the most captivating and influential figures in Greek mythology. Known for her enchanting beauty and her power to ignite passion and attraction, Aphrodite's influence extends across both the divine and mortal realms. Her myths and stories explore themes of love, lust, jealousy, and the complex nature of human relationships.

Aphrodite's Origins and Symbols

Aphrodite's origins are unique and shrouded in myth. According to the most famous version of her birth, she emerged from the sea foam near the island of Cyprus. This extraordinary birth is described in Hesiod's "Theogony," where it is said that she was born from the foam produced by Uranus's severed genitals, which Cronus had thrown into the sea. Another tradition, detailed in Homer's "Iliad," portrays her as the daughter of Zeus and the Titaness Dione.

Aphrodite's symbols include the dove, swan, and sparrow, all birds associated with love and beauty. The rose, anemone, and myrtle are her sacred plants, representing her connection to romance and passion. In art, she is often depicted with an apple, a seashell, or a mirror, reflecting her beauty and allure.

Aphrodite and the Power of Love

As the goddess of love, Aphrodite possessed an unparalleled ability to incite passion and desire among gods and mortals alike. Her powers were far-reaching, influencing romantic and sexual relationships, marriage, and even the outcome of wars.

One of the most famous stories highlighting Aphrodite's influence is the **Judgment of Paris**. When Eris, the goddess of discord, threw a golden apple inscribed "To the Fairest" among the gods, Hera, Athena, and Aphrodite each claimed it. They asked Paris, a prince of Troy, to decide who deserved the apple. Hera offered him power, Athena offered wisdom and skill in battle, and Aphrodite promised him the love of the most beautiful woman in the world, Helen of Sparta. Paris chose Aphrodite, setting off a chain of events that led to the Trojan War. This myth underscores Aphrodite's power to sway hearts and ignite conflicts.

Aphrodite's Love Affairs and Offspring

Aphrodite's own love life was as complex and passionate as the emotions she inspired. Despite being married to Hephaestus, the god of blacksmiths and craftsmen, Aphrodite had numerous lovers, both mortal and divine. Her most famous affair was with Ares, the god of war. Their union produced several children, including:

- **Eros (Cupid)**, the god of love, who wielded arrows that could make people fall in love.
- **Anteros**, the god of requited love.
- **Harmonia**, the goddess of harmony, who married Cadmus, the founder of Thebes.

Another significant lover of Aphrodite was the mortal Adonis, whose beauty captivated her. Adonis was tragically killed by a wild boar during a hunt, and his death deeply grieved Aphrodite. From his blood, she caused the anemone flower to bloom, symbolizing the transient nature of beauty and life.

Aphrodite also had a liaison with Anchises, a mortal prince of Troy. Their union produced Aeneas, a hero of the Trojan War and the legendary ancestor of the Romans. This connection underscores Aphrodite's role in both Greek and Roman mythology.

Aphrodite's Role in Human Affairs

Aphrodite's influence extended far beyond her personal relationships, affecting the lives of countless mortals. She was often called upon to bless marriages, inspire love, and bring beauty into the world. However, her involvement was not always benevolent; she could also incite jealousy, infidelity, and strife.

One notable myth illustrating Aphrodite's dual nature is the story of **Pygmalion**, a sculptor who fell in love with a statue he had created. Moved by his devotion, Aphrodite brought the statue to life, transforming it into a woman named Galatea. This myth highlights Aphrodite's power to bring love and beauty into existence.

Conversely, the story of **Hippolytus** reveals the darker side of her influence. Hippolytus, a devotee of Artemis, scorned Aphrodite and vowed to remain chaste. Angered by his rejection, Aphrodite caused his stepmother, Phaedra, to fall in love with him, leading to a tragic series of events that resulted in both their deaths. This tale underscores the potential for love to cause destruction and tragedy when manipulated by divine forces.

Aphrodite's Worship and Cultural Impact

Aphrodite was widely worshiped throughout ancient Greece, with numerous temples and festivals dedicated to her. The island of Cyprus, particularly the city of Paphos, was a major center of her cult, believed to be her birthplace. Other significant sites of worship included Cythera, Corinth, and Athens.

Festivals in her honor, such as the **Aphrodisia**, celebrated her influence over love and beauty. These festivals often included processions, sacrifices, and various rituals intended to invoke Aphrodite's blessings and favor. In Athens, her sanctuary in the Gardens was a popular place for worship and contemplation.

In art and literature, Aphrodite was depicted as the epitome of beauty and desire. Renowned works such as the "Venus de Milo" and Botticelli's "The Birth of Venus" have immortalized her image, reflecting her enduring influence on Western art and culture.

Conclusion

Aphrodite, the goddess of love, beauty, and desire, is a powerful and multifaceted figure in Greek mythology. Her stories explore the complexities of human emotions, the transformative power of love, and the fine line between passion and destruction. Through her myths, we gain insight into the ancient Greeks' understanding of love and beauty, as well as the intricate relationships between gods and mortals.

As we continue to delve into the lives of the other Olympians, Aphrodite's legacy as a goddess who embodies both the joys and sorrows of love remains a testament to the richness and depth of Greek mythology. Her stories remind us of the profound impact that love and desire can have on our lives, shaping our destinies and connecting us to the divine.

2.10 HEPHAESTUS: GOD OF FIRE

Hephaestus, the god of fire, blacksmiths, and craftsmanship, stands out among the Olympians for his skill and creativity. Unlike many of the other gods who are often depicted as flawless and majestic, Hephaestus is characterized by his physical imperfection and his role as the divine artisan. His myths and stories celebrate the value of hard work, ingenuity, and resilience.

Hephaestus's Origins and Symbols

Hephaestus's birth and origins are unique and varied across different myths. In one version, he is the son of Zeus and Hera. In another, he is born solely to Hera, who conceived him parthenogenetically (without a male consort) as a response to Zeus birthing Athena from his head. His birth was not without complication; born lame and weak, Hephaestus was cast out of Olympus by his mother Hera, who was ashamed of his deformity. Another myth suggests it was Zeus who threw him from Olympus after Hephaestus tried to intervene in a quarrel between Zeus and Hera.

Despite his rough start, Hephaestus survived and was raised by sea nymphs Thetis and Eurynome. His symbols include the anvil and hammer, representing his blacksmith skills, and the forge, a place where he worked his wonders. The donkey is also associated with him, reflecting his hard work and endurance.

Hephaestus as the Divine Blacksmith

Hephaestus's primary role in Greek mythology is that of the divine blacksmith and craftsman. His forges, often located under volcanoes, were said to be the source of his unmatched creations. Hephaestus crafted many of the gods' most powerful and iconic items, including:

- **Zeus's thunderbolts**, which he wielded as his primary weapon.

- **Poseidon's trident**, symbolizing his dominion over the seas.
- **Hermes's winged sandals and helmet**, enabling swift movement and travel.
- **Aphrodite's girdle**, which endowed the wearer with irresistible charm.

One of Hephaestus's most notable creations is the **armor of Achilles**, described in Homer's "Iliad" as a masterpiece of craftsmanship, imbued with divine power. This armor played a crucial role in the Trojan War, showcasing Hephaestus's ability to blend artistry with functionality.

Hephaestus's Marriage to Aphrodite

Hephaestus's personal life is marked by his marriage to Aphrodite, the goddess of love and beauty. This union, arranged by Zeus, was intended to balance Hephaestus's deformity with Aphrodite's beauty. However, their marriage was fraught with infidelity and tension, as Aphrodite had a well-known affair with Ares, the god of war.

The most famous story illustrating this tension involves Hephaestus crafting a fine net to catch Aphrodite and Ares in the act of adultery. He then exposed them to the other gods, who mocked the lovers. This tale underscores Hephaestus's cleverness and the complexities of his relationships, highlighting the contrast between his industrious nature and the more volatile aspects of love and desire represented by Aphrodite and Ares.

Hephaestus's Redemption and Resilience

Despite his physical imperfections and the challenges he faced, Hephaestus's resilience and skill earned him a respected place among the Olympians. His ability to transform raw materials into objects of power and beauty mirrored his own transformation from an outcast to a revered deity.

Hephaestus's return to Olympus is marked by several stories. In one, Dionysus, the god of wine and revelry, intoxicated Hephaestus and brought him back to Olympus on the back of a mule. Upon his return, Hephaestus was reconciled with Hera and resumed his role as the divine blacksmith. This return symbolizes Hephaestus's enduring strength and the acceptance of his unique contributions to the divine order.

Hephaestus's Role in Human Affairs

Hephaestus's influence extended to mortals, particularly those involved in crafts and metallurgy. As the patron god of blacksmiths and artisans, he was worshiped by craftsmen who sought his blessing for their work. His temples often included forges where blacksmiths would make offerings in hopes of receiving divine inspiration and skill.

The **Hephaisteion**, a well-preserved temple in Athens, is one of the most significant sanctuaries dedicated to Hephaestus. Located near the Agora, it served as a place of worship and a center for craftsmen, reflecting Hephaestus's integral role in the daily lives of the ancient Greeks.

Cultural Impact and Legacy

Hephaestus's legacy as the god of fire and craftsmanship endures in both mythology and cultural history. His stories celebrate the virtues of hard work, ingenuity, and resilience, providing a counterpoint to the more glamorous aspects of the other gods. He represents the power of transformation and the beauty that can arise from perceived flaws and imperfections.

In art and literature, Hephaestus is often depicted at his forge, surrounded by his tools and creations. His image as a humble, hardworking deity has resonated through the ages, inspiring artists and writers to explore themes of creativity, craftsmanship, and the human condition.

Conclusion

Hephaestus, the god of fire, blacksmiths, and craftsmanship, embodies the transformative power of skill and resilience in Greek mythology. His journey from an outcast to a revered artisan highlights the value of hard work and the beauty that can arise from imperfection. Through his myths, we gain insight into the ancient Greeks' appreciation for craftsmanship and the divine spark of creativity that resides in all of us.

As we continue to explore the lives of the other Olympians, Hephaestus's legacy as a master craftsman and resilient deity reminds us of the enduring power of skill, perseverance, and the creative spirit. His stories encourage us to find strength in our unique abilities and to recognize the potential for greatness in every individual.

2.11 HERMES: MESSENGER OF THE GODS

Hermes, the messenger of the gods, is one of the most dynamic and multifaceted deities in Greek mythology. Known for his speed, cunning, and versatility, Hermes serves as a link between the divine and mortal worlds. He is not only the herald of the gods but also the protector of travelers, thieves, and merchants, making him a figure of significant importance and intrigue.

Hermes's Origins and Symbols

Hermes is the son of Zeus and Maia, one of the Pleiades and the daughter of the Titan Atlas. He was born in a cave on Mount Cyllene in Arcadia, and from the moment of his birth, he exhibited extraordinary abilities and a mischievous nature. His rapid growth and quick wit were evident from the start, as he famously stole Apollo's cattle on the day he was born.

Hermes is typically depicted as a youthful, athletic figure, often wearing winged sandals (talaria) and a winged helmet (petasos), which symbolize his speed and ability to move freely between worlds. He carries the caduceus, a staff entwined with two serpents, which represents his role as a herald and a bringer of peace.

Hermes as the Divine Messenger

Hermes's primary role in Greek mythology is that of the messenger of the gods. He is tasked with delivering messages and guiding souls to the underworld, acting as a conduit between the divine and mortal realms. His speed and agility make him an ideal emissary, capable of traversing great distances and overcoming obstacles with ease.

One of Hermes's most notable functions is his role as a psychopomp, a guide for the souls of the dead. He leads them safely to the underworld, ensuring they reach their final destination. This role underscores his association with transition and boundaries, both physical and metaphysical.

Hermes the Trickster

Hermes is also known as the god of trickery and cunning. His cleverness and resourcefulness are central to many of his myths, highlighting his role as a trickster god who challenges norms and defies expectations. His theft of Apollo's cattle is a prime example of his mischievous nature. To cover his tracks, Hermes cleverly disguised the stolen cattle's tracks and created the first lyre from a tortoise shell, which he later gave to Apollo as a peace offering.

This story not only showcases Hermes's ingenuity but also establishes his connection to music and the arts. The lyre, which Apollo accepted, became one of his primary symbols and instruments, linking Hermes to the cultural and artistic pursuits of the Greeks.

Hermes the Protector of Travelers and Merchants

Hermes's role extends beyond his duties as a messenger and trickster. He is also the protector of travelers, ensuring their safety on journeys. As the god of roads and boundaries, Hermes is invoked by those embarking on voyages, whether for trade, exploration, or personal reasons. His symbols, such as the caduceus and the herald's staff, represent his authority over travel and communication.

Merchants and traders also revere Hermes as their patron. His association with commerce and trade highlights his importance in the economic activities of ancient Greece. The Greeks believed that Hermes blessed their transactions and protected their goods, making him an essential deity for anyone involved in commerce.

Hermes's Relationships and Offspring

Hermes's versatility and charm extend to his relationships with other gods and mortals. He is known for his numerous love affairs and offspring, reflecting his dynamic and multifaceted nature. Some of his notable children include:

- **Pan**, the god of the wild and shepherds, who inherited his father's playful and musical talents.
- **Hermaphroditus**, born from Hermes's union with Aphrodite, who possessed both male and female characteristics, symbolizing unity and duality.
- **Autolycus**, a master thief and trickster, known for his ability to steal and deceive without being caught.

Hermes's relationships and offspring often mirror his own attributes, emphasizing his role as a god of transition, adaptability, and boundary-crossing.

Hermes in Mythology and Culture

Hermes appears in numerous myths, often aiding heroes and gods with his quick thinking and resourcefulness. He played a crucial role in the story of Perseus, providing the hero with his winged sandals, a reflective shield, and guidance to defeat the Gorgon Medusa. His assistance to Perseus highlights his supportive nature and his importance in the success of heroic quests.

In the "Odyssey," Hermes aids Odysseus by giving him the herb moly to protect him from Circe's magic and later guiding the souls of the suitors to the underworld. These interventions showcase Hermes's protective and guiding roles, reinforcing his importance in Greek mythology.

Hermes's Worship and Cultural Impact

Hermes was widely worshiped across ancient Greece, with numerous shrines and statues dedicated to him. Herms, stone pillars topped with his head and adorned with phallic symbols, were placed at crossroads, boundaries, and doorways to invoke his protection and blessings. These markers were a common sight in the Greek landscape, symbolizing Hermes's pervasive influence.

Festivals such as the **Hermaea** celebrated Hermes with athletic competitions, reflecting his association with physical prowess and agility. His worship was integral to various aspects of Greek life, from travel and commerce to athletics and communication.

In art and literature, Hermes is depicted as a dynamic and youthful figure, embodying the ideals of movement, transition, and cleverness. His stories have inspired countless works, from ancient vase paintings to modern interpretations in literature and film. One example of a book where Hermes appears is "The Iliad" by Homer, where he plays the role of a messenger and guide for the gods and mortals alike.

Conclusion

Hermes, the messenger of the gods, embodies the qualities of speed, cunning, and versatility in Greek mythology. His roles as a divine messenger, protector of travelers, and patron of commerce highlight his importance in both the divine and mortal realms. Through his myths, we see the value of adaptability, cleverness, and the ability to navigate between worlds.

As we continue to explore the lives of the other Olympians, Hermes's legacy as a dynamic and multifaceted deity remains a testament to the richness and complexity of Greek mythology. His stories remind us of the importance of communication, the power of ingenuity, and the enduring spirit of exploration and transition in the human experience.

2.12 HESTIA: GODDESS OF THE HEARTH

Hestia, the goddess of the hearth, home, and domestic life, is one of the Twelve Olympians who holds a unique and vital place in Greek mythology. Despite her relatively low profile compared to other gods, Hestia's role as the guardian of the hearth and home underscores the importance of family, stability, and hospitality in ancient Greek culture. Her presence symbolizes the warmth and comfort of the home, the heart of both the household and the community.

Hestia's Origins and Symbols

Hestia is the eldest daughter of the Titans Cronus and Rhea, making her the sister of Zeus, Hera, Poseidon, Demeter, and Hades. Like her siblings, she was swallowed by Cronus at birth and later freed by Zeus. Unlike the other Olympians who were often involved in dramatic conflicts and adventures, Hestia chose a life of peaceful stability, dedicating herself to the hearth.

Her symbols are simple yet powerful: the hearth and its flame. The hearth was the center of the home in ancient Greece, providing warmth, light, and a place to prepare food. The ever-burning flame represented the continuity and stability of the household and community. In art, Hestia is often depicted as a modestly veiled woman, sometimes holding a staff or a flame, symbolizing her gentle and nurturing nature.

Hestia's Role and Attributes

Hestia's primary role is to maintain the hearth, both in the homes of mortals and in the sacred hearth of Mount Olympus. As the goddess of the hearth, she presides over domestic life, ensuring the stability and sanctity of the home. Her influence extends to the communal hearths of the city-states, where her sacred flame was kept burning as a symbol of unity and continuity.

Unlike many other gods, Hestia's attributes are characterized by her steadfastness, calmness, and dedication to peace. She represents the values of family, hospitality, and the sanctity of the home, making her an essential deity in the daily lives of the ancient Greeks.

Hestia's Vow of Chastity

Hestia is also known for her vow of chastity, which sets her apart from many of the other Olympian gods. She swore to remain a virgin forever, rejecting the advances of both Poseidon and Apollo. In return for her vow, Zeus granted her a place of honor in all the households and at every public hearth.

This vow of chastity emphasizes Hestia's commitment to purity and stability. It reflects her role as a protector of the home and family, free from the complexities and conflicts often associated with romantic entanglements.

Hestia in Mythology and Culture

While Hestia does not feature prominently in many myths, her presence is felt in the rituals and daily life of the ancient Greeks. Every meal began and ended with an offering to Hestia, acknowledging her as the protector of the hearth and the provider of sustenance. This practice highlights her integral role in the household and her constant presence in the lives of mortals.

One of the few myths involving Hestia tells of her protection from the advances of Priapus, a fertility god. As the story goes, during a feast, Priapus attempted to assault Hestia while she slept. A donkey's braying woke her, allowing her to escape and maintain her chastity. This myth reinforces her purity and the respect she commanded among both gods and mortals.

Hestia's Worship and Temples

Hestia's worship was not centered around grand temples like those of other gods but rather in the hearths of homes and public buildings. Every city-state had a public hearth dedicated to Hestia, where the sacred fire was kept burning continuously. This flame symbolized the life and vitality of the community, and its extinguishment was considered a dire omen.

In addition to the household hearth, Hestia was honored in the prytaneion, the town hall or community center, where the communal hearth was located. This space served as a gathering place for civic activities and reflected the central role of Hestia in both private and public life.

Cultural Impact and Legacy

Hestia's legacy as the goddess of the hearth and home endures in the values and practices of hospitality, family, and domestic life. Her influence extends beyond Greek mythology, resonating in the universal human experience of seeking warmth, stability, and comfort in the home.

In modern times, Hestia's attributes of peace, stability, and domesticity continue to be valued. She represents the quiet strength of the home, the importance of family bonds, and the nurturing aspects of life that are often overlooked in favor of more dramatic narratives.

Conclusion

Hestia, the goddess of the hearth, home, and domestic life, embodies the principles of stability, hospitality, and familial harmony in Greek mythology. Her role as the guardian of the hearth underscores the central importance of the home in both personal and communal life. Through her quiet yet profound influence, Hestia teaches us the value of peace, stability, and the sanctity of the domestic sphere.

As we conclude our exploration of the Twelve Olympians, Hestia's legacy as a symbol of home and hearth remains a testament to the enduring power of these foundational aspects of human life. Her stories and attributes remind us of the essential role of the home as a place of warmth, comfort, and connection, providing a stable foundation for both individuals and communities.

2.13 SUMMARY AND KEY TAKEAWAYS

Summary

In this chapter, we delved into the lives and roles of the Twelve Olympians, each of whom plays a crucial part in Greek mythology and ancient Greek culture. These gods and goddesses, residing atop Mount Olympus, represent various aspects of life, nature, and human experience. From the mighty Zeus, the king of the gods, to Hestia, the goddess of the hearth, we explored their origins, symbols, domains, and significant myths.

We began with Zeus, who wields the thunderbolt and rules the heavens, enforcing justice and order. Hera, his wife, embodies marriage and fidelity, despite her tumultuous relationship with Zeus. Poseidon, the god of the sea, controls the oceans and is known for his temperamental nature. Demeter, the goddess of the harvest, oversees agriculture and the changing seasons, deeply mourning her daughter Persephone's abduction by Hades.

Athena, born from Zeus's forehead, symbolizes wisdom and warfare strategy, while Apollo is the god of the sun, music, and prophecy. Artemis, Apollo's twin sister, is the goddess of the hunt and wilderness, known for her independence and chastity. Ares, the god of war, personifies the brutal aspects of conflict, contrasting with Athena's strategic approach.

Aphrodite, born from sea foam, embodies love and beauty, wielding power over the hearts of gods and mortals alike. Hephaestus, the god of fire and craftsmanship, creates magnificent weapons and artifacts despite his physical imperfections. Hermes, the swift messenger of the gods, protects travelers and merchants, known for his cunning and resourcefulness. Finally, Hestia, the goddess of the hearth, maintains the home and communal stability with her ever-burning flame.

Key Takeaways

Zeus: King of the Gods

- Zeus is the ruler of the heavens, wielding thunderbolts and maintaining order and justice.
- His numerous affairs and offspring play significant roles in many myths, reflecting his complex character.

Hera: Queen of the Gods

- Hera is the goddess of marriage and childbirth, often depicted as jealous and vengeful due to Zeus's infidelities.
- Despite her tumultuous marriage, she is a powerful protector of married women and family life.

Poseidon: God of the Sea

- Poseidon rules the oceans and is known for his temper, causing storms and earthquakes.
- His symbols include the trident and horses, and he plays a significant role in myths like the Odyssey.

Demeter: Goddess of the Harvest

- Demeter oversees agriculture and the fertility of the earth, deeply connected to the changing seasons.
- Her grief over Persephone's abduction by Hades explains the cycle of the seasons.

Athena: Goddess of Wisdom

- Athena embodies wisdom, strategic warfare, and crafts, born fully armed from Zeus's forehead.
- She is a protector of heroes like Odysseus and represents rationality and justice.

Apollo: God of the Sun

- Apollo is the god of the sun, music, prophecy, and healing, symbolizing harmony and enlightenment.
- He plays a crucial role in guiding and assisting heroes, and his oracle at Delphi was highly revered.

Artemis: Goddess of the Hunt

- Artemis is the goddess of the hunt, wilderness, and childbirth, known for her chastity and independence.
- She protects young women and wildlife, embodying the untamed aspects of nature.

Ares: God of War

- Ares represents the chaotic and brutal aspects of war, often depicted as impulsive and destructive.
- His relationship with Aphrodite and his frequent defeats highlight his complex and often negative portrayal.

Aphrodite: Goddess of Love

- Aphrodite embodies love, beauty, and desire, influencing romantic and sexual relationships among gods and mortals.
- Her birth from sea foam and her affair with Ares are central to her mythology.

Hephaestus: God of Fire

- Hephaestus is the god of fire, blacksmiths, and craftsmanship, known for his skill in creating divine weapons and artifacts.
- Despite his physical imperfections, he is respected for his ingenuity and resilience.

Hermes: Messenger of the Gods

- ○ Hermes is the swift messenger of the gods, protector of travelers, merchants, and thieves.
- ○ His cunning and versatility make him a vital intermediary between the divine and mortal worlds.

Hestia: Goddess of the Hearth

- ○ Hestia is the goddess of the hearth, home, and domestic life, maintaining the stability and sanctity of the home.
- ○ Her ever-burning flame symbolizes the continuity and unity of family and community.

Reflective Questions

- • How do the personalities and domains of the Olympian gods reflect the values and concerns of ancient Greek society?
- • In what ways do the myths of the Twelve Olympians illustrate the interplay between human nature and divine intervention?
- • How do the different aspects of war represented by Athena and Ares provide a more comprehensive understanding of conflict in Greek mythology?

2.14 MYTHOLOGY QUIZ 2

Test your knowledge about the Olympian gods with the following questions:

1. Who is the goddess of the hearth and home?

    A) Hera

    B) Hestia

    C) Demeter

    D) Athena

2. Which god is known for his winged sandals and helmet?

    A) Apollo

    B) Ares

    C) Hermes

    D) Hephaestus

3. Who is the god of the sea and earthquakes?

    A) Poseidon

    B) Zeus

    C) Hades

    D) Apollo

4. Which goddess vowed to remain a virgin forever?

A) Aphrodite

B) Hera

C) Artemis

D) Athena

5. Who is the father of Eros (Cupid)?

A) Hephaestus

B) Hermes

C) Ares

D) Apollo

6. Which goddess is associated with wisdom and strategic warfare?

A) Demeter

B) Athena

C) Hera

D) Artemis

7. Who is the god of fire and blacksmiths?

A) Ares

B) Hermes

C) Apollo

D) Hephaestus

Note: Answers to the quiz can be found in the "Answer Key" section in the Appendix.

CHAPTER 3:
HEROES AND MORTALS

3.1 HERACLES AND HIS TWELVE LABORS

Heracles, known to the Romans as Hercules, is perhaps the most famous hero in Greek mythology. His incredible strength, unwavering determination, and numerous adventures make him a captivating figure whose stories have been told and retold for centuries. Let's dive into the tale of Heracles and his twelve labors, a series of seemingly impossible tasks that defined his legendary status.

The Early Life of Heracles

Heracles was the son of Zeus, the king of the gods, and Alcmene, a mortal woman of great beauty and virtue. From birth, Heracles was destined for greatness, endowed with extraordinary strength and resilience due to his divine parentage. However, this divine connection also brought him immense hardship.

Hera, Zeus's wife, was infuriated by her husband's infidelity and harbored a deep-seated hatred for Heracles. From his infancy, Hera sought to destroy him. One of her early attempts involved sending two serpents to kill the infant Heracles in his crib, but even as a baby, Heracles' strength was unmatched; he strangled the serpents with his bare hands.

Despite these divine challenges, Heracles grew up to become a powerful and courageous young man, admired for his feats of strength and bravery. His early education included training in chariot driving, wrestling, archery, and music, which he mastered quickly due to his exceptional talents.

The Madness and the Mandate

Hera's relentless vendetta against Heracles culminated in a tragic moment of madness. Consumed by jealousy and rage, she struck Heracles with a fit of uncontrollable fury, causing him to kill his beloved wife, Megara, and their children. This act left Heracles devastated and filled with guilt.

Seeking redemption, Heracles visited the Oracle of Delphi, where he was told to serve King Eurystheus of Mycenae for twelve years as atonement for his crime. During this time, he was to complete twelve labors, each seemingly impossible and fraught with danger. These labors were intended not only as punishment but also as a means to rid the world of various monstrous threats.

Hera's influence was evident in these tasks, as she persuaded Eurystheus to make them as difficult as possible. Heracles, however, faced each challenge with courage, strength, and cleverness, showcasing the resilience and determination that have made his story endure through the ages.

The Twelve Labors

1. **The Nemean Lion**: Heracles's first task was to slay the Nemean Lion, a beast with an impenetrable hide. He trapped the lion in its cave and strangled it with his bare hands. He then used the lion's own claws to skin it, crafting a protective cloak from its pelt.
2. **The Lernaean Hydra**: Next, he faced the Hydra, a serpent-like creature with multiple heads that would regenerate if cut off. With the help of his nephew Iolaus, Heracles cauterized the necks to prevent regrowth and buried the immortal head under a rock.
3. **The Ceryneian Hind**: Heracles was tasked with capturing the Ceryneian Hind, a sacred deer with golden antlers. He pursued the hind for a year before finally capturing it without causing harm, demonstrating his patience and respect for divine creatures.
4. **The Erymanthian Boar**: He then had to capture the Erymanthian Boar alive. Heracles drove the boar into thick snow, immobilizing it and carrying it back to Eurystheus, who was so frightened that he hid in a large jar.
5. **The Augean Stables**: Heracles's fifth labor was to clean the Augean Stables, which housed thousands of cattle and had not been cleaned for years. Heracles rerouted two rivers to wash out the filth, completing the task in a single day.
6. **The Stymphalian Birds**: The sixth labor involved driving away the Stymphalian Birds, man-eating creatures with metallic feathers. Heracles used bronze castanets, a gift from Athena, to frighten the birds into flight and shot them down with his arrows.
7. **The Cretan Bull**: Heracles was then sent to capture the Cretan Bull, a magnificent but destructive beast. He wrestled the bull to the ground and brought it back to Eurystheus.

8. **The Mares of Diomedes**: The next task was to steal the man-eating mares of Diomedes, the Thracian king. Heracles subdued Diomedes and fed him to his own horses, which pacified them enough to be led back to Eurystheus.
9. **The Girdle of Hippolyta**: Heracles was tasked with obtaining the girdle of Hippolyta, the queen of the Amazons. Initially welcomed by Hippolyta, Hera intervened, inciting a battle. Heracles ultimately took the girdle and returned it to Eurystheus.
10. **The Cattle of Geryon**: The tenth labor involved stealing the cattle of Geryon, a three-bodied giant. Heracles defeated Geryon and his herdsman and drove the cattle back to Greece.
11. **The Apples of the Hesperides**: For the eleventh labor, Heracles was to retrieve the golden apples of the Hesperides. He enlisted the help of Atlas, who temporarily took back the burden of holding up the sky while Heracles retrieved the apples.
12. **Cerberus**: The final labor required Heracles to capture Cerberus, the three-headed guard dog of the underworld, without using weapons. Heracles wrestled Cerberus into submission and brought him to Eurystheus, completing his penance.

Reflections on Heracles's Labors

Heracles's twelve labors are a testament to human resilience and ingenuity. Each task, while seemingly impossible, was overcome through a combination of strength, cleverness, and assistance from others. It's a powerful reminder that even our greatest challenges can be conquered with determination and support.

His story teaches us that it's not just physical strength that matters, but also mental fortitude and the ability to think creatively. It's about finding ways to overcome obstacles, no matter how daunting they may seem.

Cultural Impact and Legacy

Heracles's twelve labors have left an indelible mark on Western culture. From literature and art to modern cinema, his exploits continue to inspire and entertain. The themes of redemption, perseverance, and heroism resonate across time, reminding us of the enduring power of myth.

Heracles's journey through his twelve labors embodies the human struggle against adversity. His story is a testament to the strength and resilience within us all, encouraging us to face our challenges head-on and emerge victorious.

The story of Theseus and the Minotaur is one of the most famous and enduring tales in Greek mythology. It combines adventure, bravery, and cleverness, illustrating the triumph of human ingenuity over monstrous terror. Theseus's journey to defeat the Minotaur and navigate the labyrinth is a story that has captivated audiences for centuries.

The Birth of Theseus

Theseus was the son of Aegeus, the king of Athens, and Aethra, a princess of Troezen. His conception itself is a blend of divine and mortal elements, as Aethra was visited by both Aegeus and Poseidon on the same night. This dual paternity bestowed Theseus with both royal and divine qualities. Raised in Troezen, Theseus grew up unaware of his royal heritage until he reached manhood. When he was strong enough, he lifted a heavy rock under which his father had placed his sandals and sword, symbols that would confirm his identity as Aegeus's son.

Theseus's Journey to Athens

Choosing the perilous overland route to Athens, Theseus embarked on a journey filled with dangers, determined to prove his heroism. Along the way, he faced and defeated several notorious bandits and monsters, including:

- **Periphetes**, the club-wielder, whom he overpowered and took his club as a trophy.
- **Sinis**, the pine-bender, who Theseus outsmarted and killed using his own method.
- **Sciron**, who forced travelers to wash his feet and then kicked them off a cliff to be devoured by a giant turtle. Theseus meted out the same fate to Sciron.
- **Cercyon**, a powerful wrestler, whom Theseus defeated in a wrestling match.

- **Procrustes**, the sadistic innkeeper who stretched or cut his guests to fit his iron bed. Theseus gave him a taste of his own medicine.

These exploits established Theseus as a hero even before he reached Athens, showcasing his bravery, strength, and intelligence.

The Minotaur and the Labyrinth

The most famous adventure of Theseus is his encounter with the Minotaur, a fearsome creature with the body of a man and the head of a bull. The Minotaur was born from the union of Pasiphae, wife of King Minos of Crete, and a divine bull sent by Poseidon. To contain this monstrous offspring, Minos commissioned the great inventor Daedalus to construct an elaborate labyrinth beneath his palace in Knossos.

As punishment for the death of his son Androgeus, King Minos demanded that Athens send seven young men and seven young women every nine years to be sacrificed to the Minotaur. This tribute was a symbol of Athens's subjugation and a source of great sorrow for its people.

When the time came for the third sacrifice, Theseus volunteered to be one of the tributes, determined to kill the Minotaur and end the bloodshed. Before departing, he promised his father, Aegeus, that he would change the ship's sails from black to white if he returned victorious.

Ariadne and the Ball of Thread

Upon arriving in Crete, Theseus caught the eye of Ariadne, the daughter of King Minos. Ariadne fell in love with Theseus and decided to help him. She gave him a ball of thread, which he could use to navigate the labyrinth. Tying one end of the thread at the entrance, Theseus ventured into the maze.

Deep within the labyrinth, Theseus encountered the Minotaur. Using his strength and combat skills, he managed to overpower and kill the beast. With the help of Ariadne's thread, he retraced his steps and emerged from the labyrinth victorious.

The Return to Athens

Theseus and the Athenian youths escaped Crete, taking Ariadne with them. However, their journey home was marred by tragedy. On the island of Naxos, Theseus abandoned Ariadne, either because Dionysus claimed her or due to some other reason shrouded in myth. Heartbroken, Ariadne was eventually consoled by Dionysus, who made her his immortal wife.

As Theseus approached Athens, he forgot to change the ship's sails from black to white. Seeing the black sails, Aegeus assumed his son was dead and, in his grief, threw himself into the sea, which thereafter was named the Aegean Sea. Theseus returned to find his father gone, but he ascended the throne as the new king of Athens, ushering in a period of prosperity and reform.

Personal Reflections on Theseus

The story of Theseus and the Minotaur has always fascinated me because it showcases not just physical strength, but also intelligence and compassion. Theseus's journey from an unknown youth to a celebrated hero reminds me of the challenges we all face in life and how we must use our wits as well as our brawn to overcome them.

I remember reading this myth as a child and feeling inspired by Theseus's bravery. His ability to navigate the labyrinth with Ariadne's thread taught me the importance of guidance and support from others, a lesson that has remained relevant throughout my life.

Cultural Impact and Legacy

The myth of Theseus and the Minotaur has left a lasting legacy in Western culture. It has been retold in various forms, from ancient pottery and frescoes to modern literature and films. The labyrinth itself has become a powerful symbol, representing complex problems and the journey to find solutions.

In Athens, Theseus was celebrated as a founding hero who brought about social and political reforms. He is credited with uniting the region of Attica under Athenian rule, establishing democracy, and setting the stage for Athens's golden age.

Conclusion

The tale of Theseus and the Minotaur is more than just a story of heroism; it is a narrative about courage, ingenuity, and the human spirit's ability to triumph over adversity. Theseus's journey through the labyrinth and his defeat of the Minotaur symbolize the challenges we all face in life and the importance of bravery and cleverness in overcoming them.

As we continue to explore the stories of other Greek heroes, Theseus's legacy reminds us that true heroism often lies not just in physical strength, but in the ability to think creatively and act with compassion. His adventures inspire us to face our own "monsters" with courage and resourcefulness, knowing that we too can emerge victorious from our personal labyrinths.

3.3 PERSEUS AND MEDUSA

Perseus, one of the most celebrated heroes in Greek mythology, is best known for his daring quest to slay Medusa, a fearsome Gorgon whose gaze could turn anyone to stone. His story is a classic tale of bravery, divine assistance, and cunning strategy, showing that true heroism often requires more than just physical strength.

The Birth of Perseus

Perseus was the son of Zeus and Danaë, the daughter of King Acrisius of Argos. According to the myth, an oracle warned Acrisius that he would be killed by his grandson. To prevent this prophecy from coming true, Acrisius imprisoned Danaë in a bronze chamber. However, Zeus, captivated by Danaë's beauty, visited her in the form of a golden shower, and Perseus was conceived.

When Acrisius discovered Danaë had given birth to a son, he was enraged and cast both mother and child into the sea in a wooden chest. The chest washed ashore on the island of Seriphos, where it was found by a kind fisherman named Dictys. Dictys took them in and raised Perseus as his own.

The Challenge of Polydectes

As Perseus grew up, he became known for his bravery and strength. The king of Seriphos, Polydectes, fell in love with Danaë but saw Perseus as an obstacle. To rid himself of Perseus, Polydectes devised a cunning plan. He announced his intention to marry another woman and demanded that each man in the kingdom present him with a gift. When Perseus, who had no wealth, asked what he could give, Polydectes cunningly asked for the head of Medusa, believing it would lead to Perseus's death.

Determined to protect his mother and prove his worth, Perseus accepted the seemingly impossible challenge. He set out on his perilous journey, guided by the gods and driven by his unwavering courage.

Divine Assistance

Perseus received significant help from the gods on his quest. Hermes, the messenger god, and Athena, the goddess of wisdom, provided him with essential tools and guidance. Hermes gave Perseus a pair of winged sandals, allowing him to fly. Athena provided a polished shield, which would later prove crucial in his encounter with Medusa.

Perseus also received directions to the Graeae, three old sisters who shared one eye and one tooth among them. By stealing their eye, Perseus forced them to reveal the location of the Hesperides, who possessed valuable items he needed for his quest. From the Hesperides, Perseus obtained a kibisis (a special bag to safely carry Medusa's head), a helmet of invisibility from Hades, and a sickle-shaped sword from Zeus.

The Slaying of Medusa

Armed with these divine gifts, Perseus journeyed to the lair of the Gorgons. Medusa was one of three sisters, but unlike her immortal siblings, she was mortal. Her hideous appearance and deadly gaze made her a formidable opponent. As he approached, Perseus used Athena's polished shield as a mirror to view Medusa's reflection, avoiding direct eye contact.

With careful precision, Perseus decapitated Medusa while she slept. From her severed neck sprang Pegasus, the winged horse, and Chrysaor, a giant wielding a golden sword, both fathered by Poseidon. Perseus quickly placed Medusa's head in the kibisis and fled, using his helmet of invisibility to evade Medusa's enraged sisters.

Rescuing Andromeda

On his journey home, Perseus encountered Andromeda, the daughter of Cepheus and Cassiopeia, king and queen of Ethiopia. Cassiopeia had boasted that Andromeda was more beautiful than the Nereids, angering Poseidon. To appease the god, Cepheus chained Andromeda to a rock as a sacrifice to a sea monster.

Perseus, captivated by Andromeda's beauty, offered to rescue her in exchange for her hand in marriage. Cepheus agreed, and Perseus used Medusa's head to turn the sea monster to stone, saving Andromeda. The two were married, and Andromeda accompanied Perseus back to Seriphos.

The Return to Seriphos

Upon returning to Seriphos, Perseus discovered that Polydectes had been mistreating Danaë. In a dramatic confrontation, Perseus revealed Medusa's head, turning Polydectes and his followers to stone. With the tyrant defeated, Dictys was made king, and Perseus, Danaë, and Andromeda left for Argos.

Fulfilling the Prophecy

Perseus eventually traveled to Argos to reunite with his grandfather, Acrisius. Fearing the prophecy, Acrisius fled, but fate could not be avoided. During an athletic competition, Perseus accidentally struck Acrisius with a discus, fulfilling the oracle's prophecy. Stricken with grief, Perseus buried his grandfather with honor and then chose to rule in Tiryns, leaving the throne of Argos to another.

Personal Reflections on Perseus

The story of Perseus resonates with me as a powerful example of how courage, intelligence, and divine favor can overcome even the most daunting challenges. Perseus's journey, marked by thoughtful strategy and reliance on divine tools, highlights the importance of careful planning and resourcefulness. This myth serves as a reminder that, much like Perseus facing the Gorgon, we too can conquer our own seemingly insurmountable obstacles by breaking them down, seeking guidance, and approaching them with determination. Perseus's victory encourages us to channel our inner hero, using wisdom and support to achieve our goals and navigate life's challenges.

Cultural Impact and Legacy

Perseus's tale has inspired countless works of art, literature, and modern media. His heroism and ingenuity continue to capture the imagination, from ancient pottery and Renaissance paintings to contemporary films and books. The imagery of Perseus holding

Medusa's head aloft is iconic, symbolizing triumph over the monstrous and the terrifying.

In addition to his personal legacy, Perseus is also linked to several geographical and astronomical names. The constellation Perseus, named in his honor, contains the notable variable star Algol, which represents the blinking eye of Medusa.

Conclusion

The story of Perseus and Medusa is a timeless legend of bravery, divine aid, and the triumph of good over evil. Perseus's journey is more than just a tale of heroism; it is a narrative about overcoming fear, leveraging resources, and the enduring power of courage and cleverness. As we explore other heroic figures in Greek mythology, Perseus's legacy reminds us that with the right combination of bravery, intelligence, and support, we can face and conquer our greatest challenges.

3.4 JASON AND THE ARGONAUTS

The story of Jason and the Argonauts is one of the most adventurous and thrilling tales in Greek mythology. It's a story filled with daring quests, mythical creatures, and the relentless pursuit of a seemingly impossible goal: the Golden Fleece. Jason's journey, supported by a band of heroic companions known as the Argonauts, encapsulates the spirit of exploration and the complexities of heroism.

The Birth and Early Life of Jason

Jason was the son of Aeson, the rightful king of Iolcos. However, his path to kingship was obstructed by his uncle Pelias, who usurped the throne. To protect Jason from Pelias's murderous intentions, his parents sent him away to be raised by the wise centaur Chiron. Under Chiron's tutelage, Jason grew up to be a strong and educated young man, destined to reclaim his father's throne.

The Prophecy and the Missing Sandal

A prophecy warned Pelias to beware of a man wearing one sandal. One day, as Pelias was making a sacrifice by the river, Jason arrived, having lost a sandal while helping an old woman (the goddess Hera in disguise) across the river. Recognizing the potential threat Jason posed, Pelias devised a plan to rid himself of Jason. He promised to relinquish the throne if Jason brought him the Golden Fleece, a task he believed to be impossible.

The Quest for the Golden Fleece

Determined to reclaim his rightful throne, Jason accepted the challenge and set out to gather a crew of the finest heroes in Greece. This group, known as the Argonauts (named after their ship, the Argo), included legendary figures such as Heracles, Orpheus, and Castor and Pollux.

The construction of the Argo was itself a marvel, built by the shipwright Argus with the guidance of Athena. The ship was endowed with a magical prow that could speak and provide guidance, a testament to the divine favor that accompanied the mission.

The Journey of the Argonauts

The journey of the Argonauts was fraught with peril and adventure. Among the notable challenges they faced were:

- **The Island of Lemnos**: The Argonauts landed on Lemnos, an island inhabited only by women. The women had killed their unfaithful husbands and initially feared the arrival of the Argonauts. However, they welcomed the heroes and formed relationships, delaying the journey.
- **The Harpies**: On the island of Thrace, the Argonauts encountered the blind prophet Phineus, tormented by Harpies that stole his food. The Boreads, sons of the North Wind and members of the crew, chased away the Harpies, freeing Phineus. In gratitude, Phineus provided crucial guidance for navigating future challenges.
- **The Clashing Rocks (Symplegades)**: These perilous rocks smashed together, crushing anything that tried to pass between them. Following Phineus's advice, the Argonauts sent a dove through first, observing its safe passage. Timing their own passage with the rocks' movement, they narrowly escaped destruction.

Reaching Colchis and the Challenge of the Fleece

The Argonauts finally reached Colchis, the land where the Golden Fleece was kept. King Aeëtes, ruler of Colchis, agreed to give Jason the fleece, but only if he could complete a series of near-impossible tasks:

- **Yoking the Fire-Breathing Bulls**: Jason had to yoke two fire-breathing bulls with bronze hooves and plow a field with them.

- **Sowing the Dragon's Teeth**: After plowing the field, Jason had to sow it with dragon's teeth, which sprouted into an army of warriors. Following Medea's advice, Jason threw a stone among the warriors, causing them to fight each other until none were left standing.

Medea's Role and the Escape

Medea, the daughter of King Aeëtes and a powerful sorceress, fell in love with Jason. She provided him with a magical ointment to protect him from the bulls' flames and guided him through the tasks. After completing the tasks, Jason still needed to overcome the guardian of the fleece: a sleepless dragon. Medea used her magic to lull the dragon to sleep, allowing Jason to seize the fleece.

With the Golden Fleece in hand, Jason and Medea fled Colchis, pursued by Aeëtes. Medea's cunning helped them escape, using various strategies to delay their pursuers, including the tragic dismemberment of her brother Absyrtus to slow down her father.

The Return to Iolcos

The journey back to Iolcos was as eventful as the outward voyage, filled with divine encounters and challenges. Upon their return, Jason presented the Golden Fleece to Pelias, but Pelias refused to honor his promise. In revenge, Medea tricked Pelias's daughters into killing their father, claiming she could restore his youth but instead leading to his death.

However, this act of vengeance led to Jason and Medea's exile. They settled in Corinth, where their story took a darker turn. Jason eventually abandoned Medea for the daughter of the king of Corinth, leading to Medea's infamous revenge, where she killed their children and Jason's new bride before fleeing.

Personal Reflections on Jason and the Argonauts

The story of Jason and the Argonauts intrigues me for its blend of adventure, heroism, and tragedy. It highlights the importance of perseverance and the complex interplay between destiny and choice. Jason's journey, marked by assembling a team of skilled individuals and overcoming numerous obstacles, serves as a powerful metaphor for tackling challenging projects. Just as Jason relied on the strengths and ingenuity of his Argonauts, we too can draw on the talents and collaboration of our teams to navigate difficulties and achieve success. This myth reminds us that with determination and the right allies, we can overcome even the most daunting challenges.

Cultural Impact and Legacy

The tale of Jason and the Argonauts has left a significant mark on Western culture, inspiring countless adaptations in literature, art, and film. The themes of adventure, teamwork, and the quest for a noble goal continue to resonate with audiences today.

In classical art, the journey of the Argonauts is depicted in numerous vase paintings and sculptures, highlighting key moments such as the retrieval of the Golden Fleece and the encounters with mythical creatures. In literature, the story has been retold by poets such as Apollonius of Rhodes and dramatists like Euripides, whose play "Medea" explores the darker aspects of Jason and Medea's relationship.

Conclusion

The story of Jason and the Argonauts is a timeless epic of heroism, adventure, and the quest for glory. Jason's journey, supported by his loyal companions and the cunning of Medea, exemplifies the enduring power of determination and the complexities of heroism. As we continue to explore the tales of other

Greek heroes, the legacy of Jason and the Argonauts reminds us that true heroism often involves overcoming great challenges, forging strong alliances, and facing the consequences of our actions.

3.5 ODYSSEUS AND HIS ADVENTURES

Odysseus, the legendary king of Ithaca, is one of the most complex and celebrated heroes in Greek mythology. Known for his cunning intellect, resourcefulness, and determination, Odysseus's adventures are chronicled in Homer's epic poem, the "Odyssey." His ten-year journey home from the Trojan War is filled with trials, tribulations, and encounters with gods and monsters, making his story one of the most enduring in Western literature.

The Trojan War and the Journey Home

The story of Odysseus begins with his crucial role in the Trojan War. He is most famous for devising the strategy of the Trojan Horse, which led to the fall of Troy. However, his real adventure starts after the war, as he attempts to return home to Ithaca, where his faithful wife Penelope and son Telemachus await him.

The Wrath of Poseidon

Odysseus's journey home is fraught with challenges, many of which are instigated by Poseidon, the god of the sea. Angered by Odysseus for blinding his son, the Cyclops Polyphemus, Poseidon vows to make Odysseus's journey as difficult as possible. This divine wrath sets the stage for the many trials Odysseus must endure.

The Lotus-Eaters

One of the first stops on Odysseus's voyage is the land of the Lotus-Eaters. Here, his crew consumes the intoxicating lotus fruit, which causes them to forget their desire to return home. Odysseus must forcibly drag his men back to the ship, emphasizing his role as a leader determined to see his mission through, no matter the distractions.

The Cyclops Polyphemus

Perhaps one of the most famous episodes in the "Odyssey" is Odysseus's encounter with the Cyclops Polyphemus. Trapped in the giant's cave, Odysseus and his men are at the mercy of Polyphemus, who begins eating them one by one. Using his wits, Odysseus introduces himself as "Nobody" and devises a plan to escape. He blinds the Cyclops with a heated stake and, when Polyphemus calls for help, he tells his fellow Cyclopes that "Nobody" is attacking him. This clever trick allows Odysseus and his men to escape, but it also incurs the lasting wrath of Poseidon.

Aeolus and the Bag of Winds

Odysseus's next encounter is with Aeolus, the keeper of the winds. Aeolus gives Odysseus a bag containing all the winds except the west wind, which will blow him directly home. However, just as Ithaca comes into sight, Odysseus's curious and mistrustful crew opens the bag, releasing the winds and blowing them off course. This mishap highlights the importance of trust and the devastating consequences of curiosity and disobedience.

The Laestrygonians

Continuing their voyage, Odysseus and his men reach the land of the Laestrygonians, a race of giant cannibals. The Laestrygonians destroy all of Odysseus's ships except the one he is on, further decimating his crew. This episode underscores the relentless dangers that Odysseus faces and his resilience in the face of seemingly insurmountable odds.

Circe the Enchantress

Next, the crew lands on the island of Aeaea, home to the sorceress Circe. She transforms Odysseus's men into pigs, but with the help of the god Hermes, Odysseus resists her magic and forces her to reverse the spell. Odysseus and his men stay with Circe for a year, during which she becomes his lover and advises him on the journey ahead. This relationship with Circe demonstrates Odysseus's ability to navigate complex interactions with powerful figures.

The Underworld

Following Circe's advice, Odysseus travels to the underworld to seek the prophecy of the blind seer Tiresias. In the land of the dead, Tiresias foretells the hardships that still await Odysseus and advises him on how to appease Poseidon and return home safely. Odysseus also speaks with the spirits of his fallen comrades and his mother, gaining valuable insights and reinforcing his determination to return to Ithaca.

The Sirens

One of the most iconic challenges Odysseus faces is the passage by the Sirens, whose beautiful song lures sailors to their doom. Forewarned by Circe, Odysseus has his men plug their ears with beeswax and orders them to tie him to the mast of the ship so he can hear the Sirens' song without succumbing to it. This episode showcases Odysseus's strategic thinking and self-discipline.

Scylla and Charybdis

Navigating between Scylla, a six-headed monster, and Charybdis, a deadly whirlpool, represents one of the most perilous moments of

Odysseus's journey. He chooses to sail closer to Scylla, accepting the loss of a few men to save the ship and the majority of his crew. This difficult decision highlights the harsh realities of leadership and the sacrifices it often entails.

The Cattle of the Sun God

On the island of Thrinacia, despite Odysseus's warnings, his starving men slaughter the sacred cattle of Helios, the Sun God. In retribution, Zeus sends a storm that destroys the ship, killing all of Odysseus's remaining crew. Odysseus alone survives, drifting to the island of Ogygia, where he is held captive by the nymph Calypso for seven years.

Calypso's Island

Calypso falls in love with Odysseus and offers him immortality if he stays with her. However, Odysseus longs for home and his family. After seven years, the gods intervene, and Zeus orders Calypso to release him. This part of Odysseus's journey emphasizes his unwavering commitment to his home and loved ones, despite the temptations of an easier life.

The Phaeacians and Return to Ithaca

After leaving Calypso, Odysseus is shipwrecked on the island of the Phaeacians, who welcome him and listen to the story of his adventures. Impressed by his tale, they provide him with the means to finally return to Ithaca. However, Poseidon, still seeking revenge, turns the Phaeacian ship to stone as punishment for helping Odysseus.

Upon reaching Ithaca, Odysseus disguises himself as a beggar with the help of Athena. He reunites with his son, Telemachus, and together they plot to overthrow the suitors vying for Penelope's hand. With careful planning and strategic thinking, Odysseus reveals his identity, defeats the suitors in a dramatic battle, and reclaims his home and throne.

Personal Reflections on Odysseus

Odysseus's journey resonates deeply with me because it embodies not just physical endurance but also mental and emotional resilience. His ability to navigate complex situations, make tough decisions, and stay focused on his ultimate goal is incredibly inspiring. Odysseus's perseverance in the face of adversity serves as a powerful reminder that with determination and resilience, we can overcome major life challenges and stay committed to our objectives. His story encourages us to stay focused and adaptable, no matter how difficult the journey may be.

Cultural Impact and Legacy

The adventures of Odysseus have left an indelible mark on Western literature and culture. The "Odyssey" is considered one of the greatest works of literature, influencing countless stories and adaptations. Themes of adventure, homecoming, and the hero's journey are prevalent in modern storytelling, from novels and films to television series.

Odysseus's cleverness and strategic mind have made him a symbol of human ingenuity and resilience.

Conclusion

The story of Odysseus and his adventures is a timeless epic of perseverance, intelligence, and the unwavering desire to return home. His journey through the trials and tribulations of the "Odyssey" embodies the enduring human spirit and the quest for meaning and fulfillment. As we continue to explore the tales of other Greek heroes, Odysseus's legacy reminds us that with determination, ingenuity, and resilience, we can overcome even the most daunting challenges and achieve our goals.

3.6 BELLEROPHON AND THE CHIMERA

Bellerophon, one of the lesser-known yet equally fascinating heroes of Greek mythology, is best known for his conquest of the monstrous Chimera. His story is a blend of adventure, divine intervention, and the tragic consequences of hubris. Through his exploits, Bellerophon exemplifies the complexities of heroism, showing both the heights of glory and the depths of downfall.

The Birth and Early Life of Bellerophon

Bellerophon was the son of Glaucus, the king of Corinth, and Eurynome. Some myths suggest his true father was Poseidon, the god of the sea, which would explain his extraordinary abilities and divine favor. From a young age, Bellerophon was renowned for his striking beauty and his prowess in combat.

However, his early life was marred by tragedy and misfortune. While still a young man, he accidentally killed his brother or a close relative, depending on the version of the myth. Seeking purification for his crime, he traveled to the court of King Proetus in Tiryns.

The False Accusation and Quest for Redemption

At the court of Proetus, Bellerophon found himself entangled in a dangerous situation. The king's wife, Stheneboea (also known as Anteia), fell in love with him. When Bellerophon rejected her advances, Stheneboea falsely accused him of trying to seduce her. Furious but unable to kill Bellerophon due to his guest-friendship obligations, Proetus sent him to his father-in-law, King Iobates of Lycia, with a sealed letter. The letter requested that Iobates arrange for Bellerophon's death.

Upon reading the letter, Iobates was reluctant to kill Bellerophon directly. Instead, he assigned Bellerophon a series of seemingly impossible tasks, hoping he would perish in the attempt. The first and most dangerous task was to slay the Chimera, a fearsome creature ravaging the land.

The Chimera

The Chimera was a monstrous hybrid with the head of a lion, the body of a goat, and the tail of a serpent. It breathed fire and was a symbol of chaos and destruction. Defeating such a beast seemed an impossible feat for any mortal.

Pegasus and Divine Assistance

Recognizing the enormity of the task, Bellerophon sought the favor of the gods. The goddess Athena appeared to him in a dream and advised him to seek out Pegasus, the winged horse born from the blood of Medusa. Following her guidance, Bellerophon found Pegasus drinking from the well of Pirene.

With Athena's help, Bellerophon tamed Pegasus using a golden bridle. Mounted on the magnificent winged horse, Bellerophon now had the advantage of aerial combat, allowing him to attack the Chimera from above, out of reach of its fiery breath.

The Battle with the Chimera

Bellerophon soared into the sky on Pegasus, evading the Chimera's fiery blasts. Using his agility and height advantage, he rained down arrows upon the beast. Despite its formidable nature, the Chimera was vulnerable to Bellerophon's strategic attacks. In a final move, he attached a block of lead to his spear and thrust it into the Chimera's throat. The beast's fiery breath melted the lead, causing it to flow into its body and suffocate it. The Chimera was defeated, and Bellerophon emerged victorious.

Further Adventures and Hubris

Bellerophon's triumph over the Chimera earned him great honor and recognition. However, Iobates was still not convinced of his innocence and set him further tasks: battling the Solymi tribe and the Amazons. With Pegasus, Bellerophon accomplished these feats with remarkable success.

Impressed and convinced of Bellerophon's divine favor, Iobates finally ceased his attempts to kill him. He offered Bellerophon his daughter's hand in marriage and half of his kingdom. Bellerophon's life seemed destined for continued glory and happiness.

However, success bred hubris in Bellerophon. Believing himself invincible and favored by the gods, he attempted to fly to Mount Olympus on Pegasus. This act of hubris angered Zeus, who sent a gadfly to sting Pegasus. The horse reared, throwing Bellerophon to the ground. Depending on the myth, Bellerophon either fell to his death or survived the fall but lived the rest of his life crippled and blind, wandering the earth in disgrace.

Personal Reflections on Bellerophon

Bellerophon's story has always struck me as a powerful reminder of the fine line between confidence and hubris. His initial courage and reliance on divine assistance led to incredible achievements, but his downfall underscores the importance of humility and the dangers of overreaching. This myth prompts reflection on the times in our own lives where challenges require confidence tempered with caution. In both professional and personal pursuits, Bellerophon's tale serves as a cautionary reminder to remain grounded and respectful of our limits.

Cultural Impact and Legacy

The tale of Bellerophon and the Chimera has inspired countless works of art and literature. His conquest of the Chimera is depicted in ancient pottery, sculptures, and Renaissance paintings, symbolizing the triumph of good over evil. The image of Bellerophon riding Pegasus has become iconic, representing the power of human ingenuity and the potential for greatness with divine support.

In literature, Bellerophon's story is mentioned in works by Homer, Hesiod, and Pindar, among others. His adventures have also influenced modern fantasy and storytelling, where themes of heroism, divine intervention, and the tragic flaws of heroes continue to resonate.

Conclusion

Bellerophon's story is a rich tapestry of heroism, divine favor, and the perils of hubris. His victory over the Chimera showcases his bravery and resourcefulness, while his ultimate downfall serves as a poignant reminder of the dangers of excessive pride. As we continue to explore the tales of other Greek heroes, Bellerophon's legacy reminds us that true heroism involves not only great deeds but also humility and self-awareness. His adventures inspire us to strive for greatness while remaining mindful of our limitations and respectful of the forces beyond our control.

3.7 ATALANTA: THE SWIFT HUNTRESS

Atalanta, known for her incredible speed and unmatched hunting skills, is a unique and fascinating heroine in Greek mythology. Her story is one of defiance, independence, and exceptional prowess in a world dominated by male heroes. Atalanta's adventures highlight her strength, intelligence, and determination to carve out her own destiny.

Atalanta's Origins and Early Life

Atalanta's origins are shrouded in mystery and vary across different versions of her myth. According to one version, she was the daughter of King Iasus of Arcadia and Clymene. Disappointed by having a daughter instead of a son, Iasus abandoned her on a mountainside to die. However, Atalanta was rescued and raised by a she-bear, which nurtured her as one of its own. Eventually, she was found by a group of hunters who took her in and taught her the ways of the wild.

From her early years, Atalanta exhibited extraordinary abilities. She grew up to be a swift runner and an exceptional hunter, living freely in the wilderness and gaining renown for her skills.

The Calydonian Boar Hunt

One of Atalanta's most famous adventures is the Calydonian Boar Hunt. The king of Calydon, Oeneus, had neglected to honor Artemis in his sacrifices, and as a punishment, the goddess sent a monstrous boar to ravage the land. Oeneus called upon the greatest heroes of Greece to join a hunt to kill the beast.

Atalanta was the only woman to join the hunt, and her presence initially caused some controversy among the male heroes. However, she quickly proved her worth. During the hunt, she was the first to draw blood from the boar with her arrow, and her actions led to the eventual slaying of the beast by Meleager, the leader of the hunt. Impressed by her bravery and skill, Meleager awarded her the boar's hide, causing a rift with his uncles who believed a woman should not receive such an honor. This led to further conflict, showcasing the deep-seated gender biases of the time.

Atalanta's Love and the Footrace

Despite her independence, Atalanta's beauty attracted many suitors. To avoid marriage, she devised a clever challenge: she would marry only the man who could outrun her in a footrace. Those who failed would be put to death. Confident in her unmatched speed, Atalanta defeated many suitors until a clever young man named Hippomenes (or Melanion in some versions) came forward.

Hippomenes prayed to Aphrodite for help, and the goddess provided him with three golden apples. During the race, Hippomenes used the apples to distract Atalanta. Each time she stopped to pick one up, he gained an advantage. Ultimately, the strategy worked, and Hippomenes won the race. True to her word, Atalanta married him.

The Downfall and Transformation

Although their marriage began happily, it was not without divine repercussions. One day, overcome by passion, Atalanta and Hippomenes consummated their marriage in a sacred temple, angering the gods. As punishment, they were transformed into lions and condemned to pull the chariot of the goddess Cybele for eternity. This transformation reflects the complex interplay between human actions and divine will in Greek mythology.

Atalanta's Legacy

Atalanta's story has left a lasting legacy in Greek mythology, symbolizing female strength and independence. Her prowess as a huntress and runner defied the traditional gender roles of ancient Greece, making her a role model for women and a symbol of empowerment.

Personal Reflections on Atalanta

Atalanta's story has always resonated with me as a powerful reminder of the importance of perseverance and self-reliance. Her ability to thrive in a male-dominated world and her determination to live life on her own terms are inspiring. I often think of Atalanta when facing challenges that require me to stand firm in my beliefs and rely on my own abilities.

Cultural Impact and Legacy

Atalanta's story has been depicted in various forms of art and literature throughout the centuries. Her image as a swift huntress is often featured in ancient vase paintings and sculptures, highlighting her role in the Calydonian Boar Hunt and her legendary footrace. Her story continues to inspire modern adaptations in books, films, and television, where themes of female empowerment and resilience remain relevant. One example of a modern book featuring Atalanta is "The Lost Hero" by Rick Riordan, where she appears as a mythological figure inspiring the characters with her bravery and skills.

Conclusion

Atalanta, the swift huntress, stands out as a remarkable heroine in Greek mythology. Her strength, independence, and determination to defy societal expectations make her an enduring symbol of female empowerment. Through her adventures, Atalanta teaches us the value of self-reliance, courage, and the importance of living life on our own terms. As we conclude our exploration of Greek heroes, Atalanta's legacy reminds us that true heroism knows no gender and that the pursuit of one's own destiny is a timeless and universal quest.

3.8 SUMMARY AND KEY TAKEAWAYS

Summary

In this chapter, we explored the fascinating tales of some of the most iconic heroes in Greek mythology. Each of these heroes embarked on perilous journeys, faced formidable foes, and overcame immense challenges, showcasing the timeless themes of courage, ingenuity, and the human spirit's resilience.

We began with **Heracles and His Twelve Labors**, where Heracles, driven by a need for redemption, accomplished twelve seemingly impossible tasks through sheer strength, determination, and clever thinking. His journey from a guilt-ridden hero to a demigod reflects the eternal struggle for redemption and glory.

Next, we delved into the tale of **Theseus and the Minotaur**, where Theseus's bravery and intelligence led him to slay the monstrous Minotaur and navigate the treacherous labyrinth with the help of Ariadne's thread. Theseus's story is a testament to the power of ingenuity and the importance of seeking guidance and support from others.

Perseus and Medusa followed, highlighting Perseus's courage and clever use of divine gifts to defeat the Gorgon Medusa. His adventures exemplify the hero's journey, from his humble beginnings to his triumphant return, illustrating the importance of divine favor and personal bravery.

The story of **Jason and the Argonauts** took us on a thrilling voyage for the Golden Fleece. With the help of his loyal companions and the sorceress Medea, Jason overcame numerous obstacles and treacherous challenges. His tale underscores the value of teamwork, loyalty, and the complexities of heroism and human relationships.

We then explored **Odysseus and His Adventures**, a ten-year odyssey filled with trials, tribulations, and divine interventions.

Odysseus's cunning intellect and unyielding determination to return home to Ithaca embody the essence of human perseverance and resilience.

In the story of **Bellerophon and the Chimera**, we saw Bellerophon's rise from disgrace to glory through his defeat of the Chimera. However, his eventual downfall due to hubris serves as a powerful reminder of the dangers of excessive pride and the importance of humility.

Finally, we examined the life of **Atalanta: The Swift Huntress**, whose incredible speed and hunting prowess set her apart as a unique heroine in Greek mythology. Atalanta's story of independence and defiance against traditional gender roles highlights the enduring power of self-reliance and determination.

Key Takeaways

Heracles and His Twelve Labors

- Heracles's journey from guilt to glory through his twelve labors demonstrates the themes of redemption, strength, and cleverness.
- His story underscores the importance of perseverance and the belief that even the most daunting challenges can be overcome.

Theseus and the Minotaur

- Theseus's bravery and ingenuity in defeating the Minotaur and navigating the labyrinth highlight the value of intelligence and resourcefulness.
- The support and guidance from Ariadne reflect the importance of collaboration and seeking help when faced with complex problems.

Perseus and Medusa

- ○ Perseus's use of divine gifts to defeat Medusa emphasizes the role of divine favor and clever strategy in achieving success.
- ○ His adventures illustrate the hero's journey from humble beginnings to triumph and the significance of courage in facing monstrous challenges.

Jason and the Argonauts

- ○ Jason's quest for the Golden Fleece showcases the importance of teamwork, loyalty, and the complexities of heroism.
- ○ The involvement of Medea highlights the interplay between human relationships and divine intervention in achieving heroic feats.

Odysseus and His Adventures

- ○ Odysseus's cunning and determination to return home exemplify the themes of resilience, intelligence, and the power of human perseverance.
- ○ His encounters with various trials and divine beings reflect the enduring struggle to overcome adversity and achieve one's goals.

Bellerophon and the Chimera

- ○ Bellerophon's defeat of the Chimera through divine assistance and bravery highlights the potential for human greatness.
- ○ His eventual downfall due to hubris serves as a cautionary tale about the dangers of excessive pride and the need for humility.

Atalanta: The Swift Huntress

- ○ Atalanta's strength, independence, and defiance of traditional gender roles make her a symbol of female empowerment and self-reliance.
- ○ Her adventures emphasize the importance of living life on one's own terms and the value of self-determination.

Reflective Questions

- How do the stories of these heroes illustrate the values and beliefs of ancient Greek society?
- In what ways do the challenges faced by these heroes reflect the universal human struggle against adversity?
- How do the traits of intelligence, bravery, and humility contribute to the success or downfall of these heroes?

3.9 MYTHOLOGY QUIZ 3

Test your knowledge about the heroes and their adventures with the following questions:

1. **Who helped Theseus navigate the labyrinth to defeat the Minotaur?**

    A) Hera

    B) Athena

    C) Ariadne

    D) Medea

2. **What did Perseus use to defeat Medusa?**

    A) A sword and a shield

    B) A bow and arrow

    C) A trident

    D) A spear and a mirror

3. **Who provided Jason with the means to defeat the challenges posed by King Aeëtes?**

    A) Hera

    B) Medea

    C) Athena

    D) Circe

4. **What animal raised Atalanta after she was abandoned as a child?**

   A) A lioness

   B) A she-bear

   C) A wolf

   D) An eagle

5. **What was the primary cause of Bellerophon's downfall?**

   A) Betrayal

   B) Hubris

   C) Cowardice

   D) Greed

6. **How did Odysseus avoid the Sirens' song?**

   A) By wearing earplugs

   B) By having his men tie him to the mast

   C) By sailing around their island

   D) By using a magical cloak

Note: Answers to the quiz can be found in the "Answer Key" section in the Appendix.

CHAPTER 4:
LEGENDARY MONSTERS
AND CREATURES

4.1 THE GORGONS

The Gorgons, with their terrifying visages and petrifying gaze, are some of the most iconic monsters in Greek mythology. Among them, Medusa is undoubtedly the most famous, but her sisters Stheno and Euryale also played significant roles in the myths. The Gorgons' story is one of transformation, vengeance, and the interplay between beauty and horror.

The Origins of the Gorgons

The Gorgons were born from the primordial sea deities Phorcys and Ceto. According to myth, the Gorgons lived at the edge of the known world, in a place far removed from human civilization. They were depicted as monstrous women with snakes for hair, whose gaze could turn anyone who looked at them to stone.

Medusa, the most famous of the three, had a particularly tragic backstory. Initially a beautiful maiden, Medusa was transformed into a Gorgon as a punishment by Athena. The reasons for this transformation vary, but one popular version of the myth suggests that Poseidon, the god of the sea, assaulted Medusa in Athena's temple. Enraged by this desecration, Athena cursed Medusa with a monstrous appearance and a deadly gaze.

Medusa and Perseus

Medusa's story is closely tied to that of Perseus, one of the greatest heroes in Greek mythology. King Polydectes of Seriphos, desiring to get rid of Perseus, sent him on a seemingly impossible quest to bring back the head of Medusa. With the help of Athena and Hermes, Perseus embarked on his journey, equipped with divine gifts: a polished shield, a sickle-shaped sword, winged sandals, a helm of invisibility, and a special bag to safely carry Medusa's head.

Approaching the Gorgons' lair, Perseus used the polished shield as a mirror to avoid Medusa's petrifying gaze. With careful precision, he beheaded Medusa while she slept. From her blood sprang Pegasus, the winged horse, and Chrysaor, a giant with a golden sword. Perseus placed Medusa's head in the special bag and fled, using the helm of invisibility to escape her vengeful sisters, Stheno and Euryale.

The head of Medusa continued to wield power even after her death. Perseus used it to turn his enemies to stone, including the sea monster threatening Andromeda and the wicked king Polydectes. Eventually, he gave the head to Athena, who placed it on her shield, the aegis, as a protective emblem.

Stheno and Euryale

While Medusa is often the focal point of the Gorgons' myth, her sisters Stheno and Euryale are equally intriguing. Unlike Medusa, they were immortal and equally terrifying. Although they did not share Medusa's tragic transformation, their role as protectors of their sister's lair adds depth to the myth, showing a familial bond amidst their monstrous nature.

Personal Reflections on the Gorgons

The story of the Gorgons, particularly Medusa, has always fascinated me. It's a blend of beauty, horror, and transformation, highlighting the complexity of Greek mythology. One personal reflection I have is about the concept of transformation and how it relates to our own lives. Just as Medusa's appearance was dramatically altered by divine intervention, our lives can change in an instant due to external forces beyond our control. The resilience of Medusa, even in her monstrous form, reminds me of the strength we find in ourselves when facing adversity.

It's a reminder that even our most challenging experiences can become sources of fortitude and growth.

Cultural Impact and Legacy

The Gorgons, especially Medusa, have left a lasting legacy in art, literature, and popular culture. Medusa's head is one of the most recognizable symbols from Greek mythology, appearing in countless works of art, from ancient vase paintings to Renaissance masterpieces. Her image has been used to symbolize both the protective and destructive power of the gaze.

In modern times, Medusa has been reinterpreted in various ways, often as a symbol of female rage and empowerment. Her story resonates with contemporary themes of transformation and resilience, making her a powerful figure in feminist discourse. One example of a modern interpretation is the novel "Circe" by Madeline Miller, where Medusa's story is reimagined, exploring her character with depth and empathy, highlighting themes of victimization and empowerment.

Conclusion

The Gorgons, with their fearsome appearance and tragic backstories, are a testament to the rich complexity of Greek mythology. Medusa's tale, in particular, offers profound insights into themes of transformation, vengeance, and the duality of beauty and horror. As we continue to explore the legendary monsters and creatures of Greek mythology, the Gorgons remind us of the power of myth to convey deep and enduring truths about the human experience.

4.2 THE HYDRA

The Hydra, a multi-headed serpent-like monster, is one of the most fearsome and enduring symbols in Greek mythology. Known for its regenerative ability, where cutting off one head would result in two more growing in its place, the Hydra represents the seemingly insurmountable challenges and persistent problems that one might face in life. The tale of the Hydra, primarily featured in the Labors of Heracles, highlights themes of perseverance, ingenuity, and the struggle against overwhelming odds.

The Origins of the Hydra

The Hydra, also known as the Lernaean Hydra, was said to dwell in the swamps of Lerna, a region in the Argolid. According to mythology, the Hydra was the offspring of Typhon and Echidna, making it a sibling to other monstrous creatures like Cerberus, the Chimera, and the Sphinx. The Hydra had many heads—most accounts suggest nine, but some variations mention as many as a hundred. It was also said to have poisonous breath and blood so toxic that even its scent was deadly.

Heracles and the Second Labor

The most famous story involving the Hydra is Heracles' Second Labor, one of the Twelve Labors he was tasked with completing as a penance for killing his family in a fit of madness induced by Hera. King Eurystheus, hoping to see Heracles fail, assigned him the task of slaying the Hydra.

Accompanied by his nephew Iolaus, Heracles set out to the swamps of Lerna to confront the monster. As they approached the Hydra's lair, Heracles covered his mouth and nose to protect himself from the beast's lethal fumes. Armed with a sword and shield, he engaged the Hydra, cutting off its heads. However, each decapitated head quickly regenerated, two new ones growing in place of each one severed.

The Role of Iolaus and the Final Strategy

Realizing that conventional methods would not work, Heracles enlisted the help of Iolaus. Following Athena's advice, Iolaus used a torch to cauterize each neck stump immediately after Heracles cut off a head, preventing new heads from growing. This teamwork and quick thinking were crucial in overcoming the Hydra's regenerative ability.

As they fought, Hera, who was watching from Mount Olympus, sent a giant crab to distract Heracles. Despite this additional challenge, Heracles crushed the crab under his foot and continued his assault on the Hydra. After an intense battle, Heracles finally defeated the beast by severing its immortal head, which he buried under a heavy rock to ensure it would never regenerate. He then dipped his arrows in the Hydra's poisonous blood, making them deadly weapons for future encounters.

Symbolism of the Hydra

The Hydra's story is rich with symbolism. The creature's regenerative ability represents the idea of persistent problems that seem to multiply when faced head-on. Heracles' method of cauterizing the neck stumps symbolizes the need for thorough solutions to prevent issues from recurring. The Hydra also embodies the concept of inner demons or personal challenges that require both strength and strategy to overcome.

Personal Reflections on the Hydra

The tale of the Hydra resonates deeply as a powerful metaphor for the persistent challenges we face in life. Every solution often uncovers new problems, much like the Hydra's heads. Reflecting on the Hydra's story reminds us that perseverance and strategic thinking are crucial when dealing with complex problems. It's not just about brute strength, but also about finding the right approach and seeking help when needed.

Cultural Impact and Legacy

The Hydra has left an enduring mark on popular culture and literature. Its image appears in countless artworks, from ancient pottery to modern illustrations. The Hydra's regenerative nature has become a metaphor for seemingly intractable problems in fields as diverse as politics, business, and personal development.

In modern storytelling, the Hydra often appears as a formidable opponent in fantasy literature, films, and video games. Its fearsome reputation and the dramatic nature of its defeat make it a compelling antagonist and a symbol of the hero's journey against overwhelming odds.

Conclusion

The Hydra, with its many heads and deadly nature, is a potent symbol of the persistent challenges we face in life. Heracles' triumph over the Hydra through perseverance, ingenuity, and teamwork serves as an enduring lesson in overcoming seemingly insurmountable obstacles. As we continue to explore the legendary monsters and creatures of Greek mythology, the story of the Hydra reminds us of the importance of strategy, support, and determination in the face of adversity.

4.3 THE CHIMERA

The Chimera, a fearsome and fire-breathing creature from Greek mythology, is one of the most intriguing and terrifying monsters ever conceived. This mythical beast symbolizes chaos, destruction, and the blending of different elements into a single fearsome entity. The Chimera's story, particularly its battle with the hero Bellerophon, showcases themes of bravery, divine intervention, and the triumph of good over evil.

The Origins of the Chimera

The Chimera was a monstrous creature born from the union of Typhon and Echidna, making it a sibling to other notorious creatures like the Hydra, Cerberus, and the Sphinx. According to legend, the Chimera had the body and head of a lion, a goat's head protruding from its back, and a serpent for a tail. Its fire-breathing ability added to its terrifying nature, making it a formidable opponent for anyone who dared to confront it.

The Reign of Terror

The Chimera resided in Lycia, a region in Asia Minor, where it wreaked havoc on the land and its inhabitants. Its fiery breath destroyed crops and homes, while its savage nature caused fear and panic among the people. The monster's reign of terror prompted the king of Lycia, Iobates, to seek a hero who could defeat it.

Bellerophon and the Quest

Bellerophon, a young hero with a tragic past and a thirst for redemption, was the one chosen to face the Chimera. His story is interwoven with themes of exile, false accusations, and divine favor. Sent to Lycia with a sealed message requesting his death, Bellerophon was tasked by King Iobates to slay the Chimera as a means to achieve the seemingly impossible and seal his fate.

Divine Assistance and Pegasus

Recognizing the enormity of his task, Bellerophon sought the favor of the gods. Athena, the goddess of wisdom, appeared to him in a dream and advised him to capture the winged horse Pegasus, the offspring of Poseidon and Medusa. With Athena's guidance, Bellerophon found Pegasus drinking from the spring of Pirene and managed to tame the magnificent creature using a golden bridle given to him by the goddess.

Mounted on Pegasus, Bellerophon gained a significant advantage over the Chimera. The ability to fly allowed him to attack from the air, avoiding the monster's deadly fire breath and the reach of its multiple heads.

The Battle with the Chimera

The confrontation between Bellerophon and the Chimera is one of the most dramatic in Greek mythology. Armed with a spear and shield, Bellerophon attacked the Chimera from above. He evaded the beast's fiery breath and the snapping jaws of its lion and goat heads. Using his agility and height advantage, Bellerophon rained down arrows and spear thrusts upon the creature.

In a final, ingenious move, Bellerophon attached a block of lead to the end of his spear and thrust it into the Chimera's open mouth. The beast's fiery breath melted the lead, causing it to flow down its throat and solidify, choking the creature and extinguishing its life. The Chimera's defeat marked the end of its reign of terror and cemented Bellerophon's status as a hero.

Symbolism of the Chimera

The Chimera represents a combination of different elements—lion, goat, and serpent—fused into one monstrous entity. This amalgamation symbolizes the chaos and unpredictability of nature and life itself. The creature's fire-breathing ability further emphasizes its destructive power and the formidable challenges that one might face.

Bellerophon's victory over the Chimera symbolizes the triumph of order over chaos, courage over fear, and ingenuity over brute strength. The story also highlights the importance of divine favor and assistance in overcoming seemingly insurmountable obstacles.

Personal Reflections on the Chimera

The story of the Chimera resonates as a powerful metaphor for the complex challenges we encounter in life. Like Bellerophon, tackling such challenges often requires devising a creative strategy and relying on support from others. The tale of the Chimera reminds us that with ingenuity, courage, and teamwork, even the most daunting challenges can be overcome.

Cultural Impact and Legacy

The Chimera has left an indelible mark on art, literature, and popular culture. Its fearsome image appears in countless works of art, from ancient Greek pottery to Renaissance paintings and modern illustrations. The term "chimera" has also entered the lexicon as a metaphor for something composed of disparate elements or an impossible fantasy.

In contemporary storytelling, the Chimera often features as a formidable opponent in fantasy literature, films, and video games. Its terrifying nature and dramatic defeat make it a compelling symbol of the hero's journey and the struggle against overwhelming odds. For instance, in the popular video game "God of War III," the Chimera is one of the monstrous foes that the protagonist, Kratos, must battle. This depiction highlights the creature's fearsome attributes and serves as a significant challenge in Kratos's epic quest. Similarly, in Rick Riordan's "Percy Jackson & the Olympians" series, the Chimera is portrayed as a menacing adversary that the young hero, Percy, must confront, further emphasizing the creature's role as a symbol of formidable challenges in the hero's journey.

Conclusion

The Chimera, with its terrifying appearance and destructive power, is a potent symbol of chaos and the complex challenges we face in life. Bellerophon's triumph over the Chimera through bravery, ingenuity, and divine assistance serves as an enduring lesson in overcoming seemingly insurmountable obstacles. As we continue to explore the legendary monsters and creatures of Greek mythology, the story of the Chimera reminds us of the importance of creativity, courage, and the support of others in our own battles against the "monsters" we encounter.

4.4 THE CYCLOPS

The Cyclops, one-eyed giants of Greek mythology, are some of the most memorable and intimidating creatures in ancient stories. Known for their immense strength and fearsome appearance, Cyclopes played significant roles in various myths, most notably in the adventures of Odysseus. The stories of these giants explore themes of power, cunning, and the relationship between humans and the divine.

The Origins and Types of Cyclops

Cyclopes, meaning "circle-eyed," are generally categorized into two distinct groups: the primordial Cyclopes and the Cyclopes of later myths.

- **Primordial Cyclopes**: These were the children of Uranus (Sky) and Gaia (Earth). Named Brontes, Steropes, and Arges, these Cyclopes were known for their craftsmanship and were the forgers of Zeus's thunderbolts, Poseidon's trident, and Hades's helm of darkness. Their skills made them invaluable to the gods during the Titanomachy, the war between the Titans and the Olympians.
- **Homeric Cyclopes**: These Cyclopes are depicted differently, notably in Homer's "Odyssey." They are portrayed as savage shepherds living on an isolated island, with Polyphemus being the most famous among them. These Cyclopes are not associated with craftsmanship but are known for their brutish nature and hostility towards humans.

Polyphemus and Odysseus

The most famous encounter with a Cyclops is that of Odysseus and Polyphemus in the "Odyssey." After the Trojan War, Odysseus and his men, seeking refuge, landed on the island of the Cyclopes. They discovered a cave filled with provisions and decided to take shelter there, unaware that it belonged to Polyphemus.

When Polyphemus returned and found the intruders, he trapped them in the cave by rolling a massive stone across the entrance. He began to eat Odysseus's men one by one, demonstrating his savage nature and immense strength. Odysseus, known for his cleverness, devised a plan to escape.

The Plan to Escape

Odysseus introduced himself to Polyphemus as "Nobody." He then offered the Cyclops strong wine, which Polyphemus greedily drank, causing him to fall into a deep, inebriated sleep. Seizing the opportunity, Odysseus and his men sharpened a large stake and drove it into Polyphemus's single eye, blinding him.

When Polyphemus awoke and cried out in pain, the other Cyclopes on the island asked who was harming him. Polyphemus replied, "Nobody is hurting me," leading them to believe he was not in danger. This clever use of words allowed Odysseus and his men to avoid immediate detection.

To escape the cave, Odysseus tied his men to the undersides of Polyphemus's sheep. When the blind Cyclops let his flock out to graze, he felt only the tops of the sheep, allowing Odysseus and his men to slip away unnoticed. This brilliant plan highlighted Odysseus's ingenuity and resourcefulness.

The Curse of Polyphemus

As Odysseus and his men sailed away, he could not resist revealing his true identity to Polyphemus, shouting it back to the shore. Enraged, Polyphemus called upon his father, Poseidon, to curse Odysseus. This curse caused many of the subsequent trials and tribulations Odysseus faced on his journey home, demonstrating the far-reaching consequences of hubris.

Symbolism of the Cyclops

The Cyclopes, particularly in the story of Polyphemus, symbolize brute force and savagery contrasted with human cunning and intelligence. The one-eyed giants, with their immense strength, represent obstacles that cannot be overcome by physical power alone but require cleverness and strategic thinking.

Polyphemus's blindness also serves as a metaphor for the dangers of ignorance and the limitations of brute strength without wisdom. Odysseus's escape from the Cyclops's cave illustrates the triumph of intellect over sheer force.

Personal Reflections on the Cyclops

The story of the Cyclops has always fascinated me because it underscores the importance of wit and strategy in overcoming challenges. Much like Odysseus, tackling seemingly insurmountable problems requires thinking creatively and devising a plan that uses available resources in unexpected ways. This story reminds us that intelligence and cleverness can often achieve what brute force cannot.

Cultural Impact and Legacy

The Cyclopes have left a lasting legacy in art, literature, and popular culture. Their image appears in ancient Greek pottery, sculptures, and frescoes, often depicting their encounters with gods and heroes. The story of Polyphemus and Odysseus has been retold in countless adaptations, from classical plays to modern films and novels. For instance, the 1997 TV miniseries "The Odyssey" vividly brings to life the encounter between Odysseus and the Cyclops Polyphemus, capturing the drama and peril of this iconic mythological episode.

In contemporary culture, the Cyclops continues to be a symbol of formidable obstacles that require cunning to overcome. The term "cyclopean" is used to describe massive stonework, reflecting the association with the Cyclopes' mythical construction abilities.

Conclusion

The Cyclopes, with their immense strength and fearsome appearance, are powerful symbols of the challenges that require more than just physical power to overcome. The story of Odysseus and Polyphemus highlights the importance of cleverness, strategic thinking, and the far-reaching consequences of one's actions. As we continue to explore the legendary monsters and creatures of Greek mythology, the tale of the Cyclops reminds us that intelligence and resourcefulness are often our greatest tools in the face of seemingly insurmountable odds.

4.5 CENTAURS AND SATYRS

Centaurs and Satyrs are two distinct groups of mythical creatures in Greek mythology, each embodying different aspects of the natural world and human nature. Centaurs, with their dual nature, represent the tension between civilization and savagery, while Satyrs symbolize the hedonistic and carefree side of humanity. Their stories and characteristics provide rich insights into the complexities of human behavior and the ancient Greek understanding of the world.

Centaurs: Half-Man, Half-Horse

Centaurs are mythical beings with the upper body of a human and the lower body of a horse. They are often depicted as wild and unruly, representing the untamed forces of nature. The duality of their form—human intelligence combined with animalistic instincts—makes them fascinating symbols of the conflict between reason and passion.

The Origin of Centaurs

According to myth, the first Centaur was born from Ixion, a king who fell in love with Hera. Zeus, aware of Ixion's intentions, created a cloud in the shape of Hera, called Nephele, to deceive him. Ixion mated with Nephele, and from this union came Centaurus, who fathered the race of Centaurs by mating with the mares of Thessaly.

Notable Centaurs in Mythology

- **Chiron**: Unlike his wild and unruly brethren, Chiron is depicted as wise, kind, and highly knowledgeable in medicine and the arts. He was a mentor to many Greek heroes, including Achilles, Asclepius, and Heracles. Chiron's wisdom and healing abilities set him apart from other Centaurs, making him a symbol of the positive potential of the blend between humanity and nature.

- **Nessus**: Another famous Centaur, Nessus is known for his encounter with Heracles. Nessus attempted to abduct Deianira, Heracles' second wife, and was shot by Heracles with a poisoned arrow. As he lay dying, Nessus deceived Deianira into taking some of his blood, claiming it would ensure Heracles' fidelity. In reality, the blood was poisoned and later led to Heracles' death, illustrating the deceitful and dangerous aspects of Centaurs.

The Battle with the Lapiths

One of the most famous myths involving Centaurs is their battle with the Lapiths at the wedding of Pirithous, king of the Lapiths. The Centaurs, invited as guests, became drunk and attempted to abduct the bride and other female guests. This led to a violent conflict, symbolizing the struggle between civilized society and barbaric impulses. The Lapiths ultimately triumphed, but the battle left a lasting impression on Greek mythology and art.

Satyrs: Followers of Dionysus

Satyrs are mythological creatures associated with Dionysus, the god of wine, revelry, and fertility. They are often depicted as part human, part goat, with the legs, tail, and sometimes the horns of a goat. Satyrs embody the carefree, hedonistic, and often mischievous aspects of human nature, indulging in music, dance, and the pleasures of the senses.

The Characteristics of Satyrs

Satyrs are typically portrayed as jovial and playful, often engaging in music and dance. They are known for their love of wine, their pursuit of nymphs, and their participation in the Bacchanalia—wild, festive celebrations in honor of Dionysus. The most notable Satyr in mythology is Silenus, a companion and tutor to Dionysus, often depicted as older and wiser, yet still fond of revelry.

Satyrs in Mythology

- **Silenus**: As the tutor and companion of Dionysus, Silenus is a prominent figure among the Satyrs. He is often depicted as an older, rotund Satyr with a fondness for wine. Despite his drunkenness, Silenus possesses wisdom and prophetic abilities, often sharing insights and guidance with Dionysus and others.
- **Marsyas**: A Satyr known for his musical prowess, Marsyas challenged Apollo to a music contest, playing the flute against Apollo's lyre. The Muses judged Apollo the winner, and Marsyas was punished for his hubris by being flayed alive. This story highlights the tension between the free-spirited nature of Satyrs and the disciplined, refined artistry of the gods.

Symbolism of Centaurs and Satyrs

Centaurs and Satyrs represent different aspects of human nature and the natural world. Centaurs embody the duality of civilization and savagery, showcasing the struggle between rational thought and primal instincts. Their stories often illustrate the consequences of giving in to base desires and the potential for harmony when reason prevails, as seen in the figure of Chiron.

Satyrs, on the other hand, symbolize the hedonistic and carefree side of humanity. They remind us of the joys of life, the importance of celebration, and the need to balance work with play. However, their tales also warn of the dangers of excess and the consequences of overindulgence, as illustrated by Marsyas's fate.

Personal Reflections on Centaurs and Satyrs

The myths of Centaurs and Satyrs have always fascinated me because they capture the complexity of human nature. The Centaurs' struggle between their wild instincts and the potential for wisdom mirrors our own efforts to balance professional responsibilities with personal fulfillment. Similarly, the Satyrs' love of revelry reminds us to find joy in the present moment while also being mindful of the consequences of excess. The story of Chiron, in particular, inspires the need to balance work with moments of relaxation and creativity, allowing for renewed energy and perspective when facing demanding challenges.

Cultural Impact and Legacy

Centaurs and Satyrs have left a lasting legacy in art, literature, and popular culture. Their images appear in ancient Greek pottery, sculptures, and frescoes, often depicting their roles in mythological tales and festivals. In Renaissance art, Centaurs and Satyrs were popular subjects, symbolizing the interplay between reason and passion.

In contemporary culture, these mythical creatures continue to inspire stories, films, and games. They represent the enduring fascination with the complexities of human nature and the relationship between civilization and the natural world. For instance, the film "The Chronicles of Narnia: The Lion, the Witch and the Wardrobe" features both Centaurs and Satyrs, portraying them as noble warriors and mischievous woodland beings, respectively. This film highlights how these ancient myths continue to captivate modern audiences and explore timeless themes.

Conclusion

Centaurs and Satyrs, with their distinct characteristics and symbolic meanings, offer rich insights into the dualities of human nature. The stories of these mythical creatures explore the balance between reason and instinct, the joys of life, and the consequences of excess. As we continue to delve into the legendary monsters and creatures of Greek mythology, the tales of Centaurs and Satyrs remind us of the importance of harmony, wisdom, and the celebration of life's pleasures.

4.6 THE NEMEAN LION

The Nemean Lion, a fearsome beast in Greek mythology, is best known for its invulnerability and its encounter with Heracles (Hercules) during his Twelve Labors. This monstrous lion symbolizes the ultimate challenge of strength and courage, as its near-impenetrable hide made it an extraordinary adversary. The story of the Nemean Lion and Heracles' triumph over it is a testament to ingenuity, bravery, and the timeless battle between man and nature.

The Origins of the Nemean Lion

The Nemean Lion was said to be the offspring of Typhon and Echidna, two of the most formidable creatures in Greek mythology, or alternatively born of the moon goddess Selene. It terrorized the region of Nemea, preying upon livestock and humans alike. The lion's hide was impervious to all weapons, making it an unstoppable force and a source of dread for the inhabitants of Nemea.

Heracles and the First Labor

The story of the Nemean Lion is most famously linked to Heracles, the greatest of Greek heroes. As part of his Twelve Labors, assigned by King Eurystheus, Heracles was tasked with slaying the Nemean Lion and bringing back its hide. This labor was designed to be nearly impossible due to the lion's invulnerability.

Upon arriving in Nemea, Heracles quickly realized that his usual weapons were ineffective against the lion's tough hide. His arrows bounced off, and his sword could not penetrate its skin. This realization forced Heracles to rely on his immense strength and cunning to defeat the beast.

The Battle with the Nemean Lion

Heracles tracked the lion to its cave, which had two entrances. Blocking one entrance to prevent the lion's escape, he entered the cave through the other. Confronting the lion in its lair, Heracles engaged in a fierce hand-to-paw combat. Using his incredible strength, he managed to wrestle the lion to the ground and, in a display of sheer power, strangled it with his bare hands.

This victory over the Nemean Lion showcased not only Heracles' physical prowess but also his adaptability and intelligence in overcoming a seemingly insurmountable challenge.

Skinning the Lion

After slaying the Nemean Lion, Heracles faced another challenge: skinning the beast to bring back its hide as proof of his conquest. Traditional tools were useless against the lion's impenetrable skin. According to some versions of the myth, Athena advised Heracles to use the lion's own claws to cut through its hide. This clever solution allowed Heracles to successfully flay the beast.

Heracles donned the lion's hide as a cloak, wearing its head as a helmet. This iconic image of Heracles wearing the Nemean Lion's pelt became a symbol of his strength and heroism, offering him additional protection in his future labors.

Symbolism of the Nemean Lion

The Nemean Lion represents the formidable and often seemingly insurmountable challenges that one encounters in life. Its invulnerable hide symbolizes obstacles that cannot be overcome through conventional means, requiring ingenuity and adaptability. Heracles' victory over the lion illustrates the triumph of human strength, courage, and cleverness in the face of overwhelming odds.

Personal Reflections on the Nemean Lion

The story of the Nemean Lion has always inspired me, serving as a powerful metaphor for overcoming significant challenges. Like Heracles, facing daunting tasks often requires thinking creatively and using unconventional methods to achieve success. This story reminds us that with determination and ingenuity, even the toughest challenges can be conquered.

Cultural Impact and Legacy

The Nemean Lion has left a lasting impact on art, literature, and popular culture. Its image appears in ancient Greek pottery, sculptures, and frescoes, often depicting Heracles' struggle and ultimate victory. This story has been retold in various forms, from classical literature to modern adaptations in films and books, such as Rick Riordan's "The Heroes of Olympus" series, which highlights the enduring appeal of Heracles' heroism.

In contemporary culture, the Nemean Lion continues to symbolize formidable challenges and the strength required to overcome them. It serves as a reminder of the power of courage and the importance of creative problem-solving in the face of adversity.

Conclusion

The Nemean Lion, with its invulnerable hide and terrifying presence, is a powerful symbol of the ultimate challenges we face in life. Heracles' triumph over the beast through strength, courage, and cleverness offers an enduring lesson in overcoming seemingly insurmountable obstacles. As we continue to explore the legendary monsters and creatures of Greek mythology, the story of the Nemean Lion reminds us of the importance of resilience, adaptability, and the indomitable human spirit.

4.7 THE SPHINX

The Sphinx is one of the most enigmatic and captivating creatures in Greek mythology. Known for its riddles and its role in the story of Oedipus, the Sphinx symbolizes mystery, wisdom, and the peril of unsolved puzzles. With the body of a lion, the wings of an eagle, and the head of a woman, the Sphinx combines elements of strength, power, and intellect, challenging those who encounter it to match its cleverness.

The Origins of the Sphinx

The Sphinx is often associated with ancient Egypt, where it is depicted as a guardian figure, but the Greek Sphinx has distinct characteristics and mythological significance. In Greek mythology, the Sphinx was sent by the gods—specifically Hera, or in some versions, Apollo—to punish the city of Thebes. It was said to be the offspring of Typhon and Echidna, like many other fearsome creatures in Greek myths.

The Riddle of the Sphinx

The Sphinx settled on a rock near the city of Thebes, where it would challenge passersby with a riddle. The riddle of the Sphinx is one of the most famous in all of mythology:

"What walks on four legs in the morning, two legs at noon, and three legs in the evening?"

Failure to answer the riddle correctly resulted in death, as the Sphinx would devour those who could not solve its puzzle. This led to widespread fear and despair in Thebes, as many failed to solve the riddle and met their end at the hands of the Sphinx.

Oedipus and the Sphinx

The Sphinx's reign of terror continued until Oedipus, a young and clever prince, arrived in Thebes. Determined to rid the city of its tormentor, Oedipus approached the Sphinx and accepted its challenge. He pondered the riddle and answered:

"Man—who crawls on all fours as a baby, walks on two legs as an adult, and uses a cane in old age."

Upon hearing the correct answer, the Sphinx was defeated. In some versions of the myth, the Sphinx threw itself from its perch to its death; in others, it simply vanished, its purpose fulfilled. Oedipus's triumph over the Sphinx not only saved Thebes but also marked the beginning of his tragic journey, as he later discovered his true identity and the horrific fate that awaited him.

Symbolism of the Sphinx

The Sphinx is rich in symbolism, representing the intersection of wisdom, mystery, and the unknown. Its riddle embodies the human quest for knowledge and understanding, as well as the perils of ignorance. The Sphinx's ability to pose a question that reflects the stages of human life also highlights the themes of growth, change, and the passage of time.

The defeat of the Sphinx by Oedipus underscores the power of intellect and insight over brute force. It suggests that the greatest challenges can often be overcome through cleverness and understanding rather than physical strength.

Personal Reflections on the Sphinx

The story of the Sphinx has always intrigued me because of its emphasis on wisdom and the importance of solving life's puzzles. Much like Oedipus, facing particularly challenging problems often requires careful thought and a deeper understanding of the underlying issues. This story teaches us the value of patience and intellectual effort in overcoming obstacles.

Cultural Impact and Legacy

The Sphinx has left a profound impact on both ancient and modern culture. Its image and story have been depicted in countless works of art, from ancient Greek pottery and sculptures to

Renaissance paintings and modern literature. The Sphinx's riddle has become a metaphor for complex problems and the quest for knowledge.

In contemporary culture, the Sphinx continues to be a symbol of mystery and wisdom. It appears in various forms of media, including films, television shows, and video games, often serving as a guardian or a challenge for heroes to overcome. For instance, the Sphinx appears in the TV show "Hercules: The Legendary Journeys," where it interacts with the protagonist in storylines inspired by Greek mythology.

Conclusion

The Sphinx, with its blend of strength, power, and intellect, remains one of the most compelling creatures in Greek mythology. Its riddle challenges us to think deeply and seek understanding, reminding us that wisdom and knowledge are our greatest tools in overcoming life's mysteries. As we continue to explore the legendary monsters and creatures of Greek mythology, the story of the Sphinx encourages us to embrace the power of intellect and the pursuit of knowledge in our own lives.

4.8 SUMMARY AND KEY TAKEAWAYS

Summary

In this chapter, we explored some of the most fascinating and terrifying creatures in Greek mythology, each embodying unique aspects of human fears and challenges. These legendary monsters and creatures not only serve as formidable opponents for heroes but also symbolize deeper themes of the human experience.

We began with **The Gorgons**, focusing on Medusa and her transformation from a beautiful maiden to a fearsome monster. Her story, intertwined with that of Perseus, illustrates themes of transformation, vengeance, and the duality of beauty and horror.

Next, we examined **The Hydra**, a multi-headed serpent that Heracles faced in his Second Labor. The Hydra's regenerative ability represents persistent problems and challenges, and Heracles' victory through ingenuity and teamwork highlights the importance of strategy and perseverance.

The Chimera, a fire-breathing hybrid creature, was conquered by Bellerophon with the help of the winged horse Pegasus. This tale underscores the triumph of bravery and ingenuity over chaos and destruction.

The Cyclops were explored through the story of Polyphemus and Odysseus. These one-eyed giants symbolize brute strength and savagery, contrasted with the cunning and cleverness of human intellect. Odysseus's escape from Polyphemus showcases the power of wit over force.

Centaurs and Satyrs represent the duality of human nature and the interplay between civilization and primal instincts. Centaurs, with their blend of human and horse, embody the tension between reason and savagery. Satyrs, followers of Dionysus, symbolize hedonism and the pursuit of pleasure, reminding us of the importance of balance in life.

The story of **The Nemean Lion** highlighted Heracles' strength and ingenuity in overcoming an invulnerable beast. The lion's hide, which could not be penetrated by conventional weapons, symbolizes seemingly insurmountable challenges that require creativity and determination to overcome.

Finally, we delved into the tale of **The Sphinx**, a creature that posed a deadly riddle to travelers. Oedipus's successful answer to the Sphinx's riddle exemplifies the triumph of intellect and wisdom over brute strength, emphasizing the importance of knowledge and understanding in solving life's puzzles.

Key Takeaways

The Gorgons

- Medusa's story highlights themes of transformation, vengeance, and the duality of beauty and horror.
- Perseus's victory over Medusa showcases the power of bravery and divine assistance.

The Hydra

- The Hydra symbolizes persistent challenges that require strategy and perseverance to overcome.
- Heracles' use of ingenuity and teamwork to defeat the Hydra underscores the importance of clever problem-solving.

The Chimera

- The Chimera represents chaos and the blending of different elements into a single monstrous entity.
- Bellerophon's victory with Pegasus highlights the triumph of bravery and ingenuity over formidable obstacles.

The Cyclops

- The Cyclopes, particularly Polyphemus, symbolize brute strength and savagery.
- Odysseus's clever escape from Polyphemus showcases the power of wit and intelligence over sheer force.

Centaurs and Satyrs

- Centaurs embody the tension between civilization and primal instincts, while Satyrs symbolize hedonism and the pursuit of pleasure.
- Their stories remind us of the complexities of human nature and the importance of balance.

The Nemean Lion

- The Nemean Lion's invulnerable hide represents seemingly insurmountable challenges.
- Heracles' victory through creativity and determination emphasizes the importance of resilience and ingenuity.

The Sphinx

- The Sphinx symbolizes mystery, wisdom, and the perils of unsolved puzzles.
- Oedipus's success in answering the Sphinx's riddle highlights the value of intellect and understanding in overcoming challenges.

Reflective Questions

- How do the stories of these mythical creatures illustrate the importance of intelligence, strategy, and perseverance in overcoming challenges?
- In what ways do these creatures symbolize the different aspects of human nature and the natural world?

- How can the lessons from these myths inspire us to approach our own problems and challenges with creativity and determination?

4.9 MYTHOLOGY QUIZ 4

Test your knowledge about the legendary monsters and creatures of Greek mythology with the following questions:

1. **Which hero defeated the Gorgon Medusa?**

    A) Theseus

    B) Heracles

    C) Perseus

    D) Odysseus

2. **How did Heracles prevent the Hydra's heads from regenerating?**

    A) By freezing the neck stumps

    B) By burning the neck stumps

    C) By covering the neck stumps with clay

    D) By using a magical potion

3. **What unique feature did the Chimera possess?**

    A) It had three heads: a lion, a goat, and a serpent

    B) It could turn people to stone with its gaze

    C) It could regenerate its limbs

    D) It had wings and could fly

4. **Who was the Cyclops that Odysseus encountered and outwitted?**

   A) Brontes

   B) Steropes

   C) Arges

   D) Polyphemus

5. **What was the notable feature of Centaurs in Greek mythology?**

   A) They had the head of a lion and the body of a man

   B) They had the body of a lion and the wings of an eagle

   C) They had the upper body of a human and the lower body of a horse

   D) They had the lower body of a human and the upper body of a serpent

6. **Which Centaur was known for his wisdom and for being a mentor to many Greek heroes?**

   A) Nessus

   B) Chiron

   C) Pholus

   D) Eurystheus

7. **How did Heracles defeat the Nemean Lion?**

    A) By using a magical sword

    B) By strangling it with his bare hands

    C) By trapping it in a net

    D) By shooting it with a poisoned arrow

8. **What riddle did the Sphinx pose to travelers?**

    A) What has roots as nobody sees, is taller than trees, up, up it goes, and yet never grows?

    B) What is so fragile that saying its name breaks it?

    C) What walks on four legs in the morning, two legs at noon, and three legs in the evening?

    D) What has a heart that doesn't beat?

9. **What did Oedipus do to defeat the Sphinx?**

    A) He fought and killed it

    B) He answered its riddle correctly

    C) He used a magical charm to make it disappear

    D) He tricked it into falling off a cliff

10. **What did Heracles use to skin the Nemean Lion?**

    A) A special knife given by Athena

    B) The lion's own claws

    C) A bronze dagger

D) His bare hands

Note: Answers to the quiz can be found in the "Answer Key" section in the Appendix.

CHAPTER 5:
MYTHS OF LOVE AND TRAGEDY

5.1 ORPHEUS AND EURYDICE

The myth of Orpheus and Eurydice is one of the most poignant and enduring love stories in Greek mythology. It captures the power of love, the pain of loss, and the bittersweet nature of hope. Orpheus, a legendary musician, and Eurydice, his beloved wife, face the ultimate test of their love when fate tears them apart.

The Love of Orpheus and Eurydice

Orpheus, the son of the Muse Calliope and the god Apollo, was blessed with extraordinary musical talent. His ability to play the lyre and sing with unmatched beauty could enchant anyone who heard him, from wild animals to trees and even the gods themselves. Eurydice, a beautiful nymph, fell deeply in love with Orpheus, and they were soon married, living a blissful life together.

The Tragic Death of Eurydice

Their happiness was short-lived. One day, while walking through a meadow, Eurydice was bitten by a venomous snake and died instantly. Orpheus was devastated by the loss of his beloved wife. Consumed by grief, he resolved to do the unthinkable: journey to the underworld and bring Eurydice back to the land of the living.

The Descent to the Underworld

With his lyre in hand, Orpheus descended into the dark and foreboding realm of Hades, the god of the underworld. His music, filled with sorrow and longing, softened the hearts of the fearsome guardians of the underworld, including Charon, the ferryman of the River Styx, and the three-headed dog Cerberus. Even the Furies, spirits of vengeance, were moved to tears by Orpheus's lament.

Orpheus's music reached the ears of Hades and Persephone, the rulers of the underworld. Intrigued and touched by his mournful melodies, they summoned Orpheus to hear his plea. Orpheus implored them to return Eurydice to him, singing of his undying love and the pain of their separation. Moved by his devotion, Hades and Persephone agreed to let Eurydice return to the living world—but with one condition.

The Test of Trust

Eurydice would follow Orpheus back to the surface, but he was forbidden to look back at her until they had both fully emerged from the underworld. If he did, she would be lost to him forever. Overjoyed, Orpheus began the journey back, trusting that Eurydice was right behind him.

As they neared the exit of the underworld, doubt and anxiety crept into Orpheus's heart. He could not hear Eurydice's footsteps and feared that she might not be there. Just before reaching the surface, Orpheus succumbed to his doubts and turned to look at Eurydice. In that fateful moment, she was pulled back into the depths of the underworld, her final farewell echoing in Orpheus's ears.

The Aftermath

Orpheus was left heartbroken and desolate. He had lost Eurydice for a second time, this time through his own actions. He wandered the earth in mourning, his music now filled with an even deeper sorrow. Eventually, he met a tragic end, but his lyre and his songs continued to resonate, immortalizing his love and loss.

Personal Reflections on Orpheus and Eurydice

The story of Orpheus and Eurydice has always resonated with me because it illustrates the profound depth of love and the devastating pain of loss. One personal reflection that comes to mind is the importance of trust in relationships. Orpheus's doubt led to his ultimate failure, reminding us that trust and faith in our loved ones are crucial, even when faced with uncertainty.

This myth also speaks to the idea of hope and the lengths we are willing to go to for the ones we love. Orpheus's journey to the underworld is a testament to the power of love and the hope that can drive us to achieve the impossible, even when the odds are stacked against us.

Cultural Impact and Legacy

The myth of Orpheus and Eurydice has inspired countless works of art, literature, music, and film. From ancient Greek pottery and Roman frescoes to modern operas and ballets, their story continues to captivate audiences. Orpheus's descent to the underworld has become a powerful metaphor for love's endurance and the human condition's resilience.

In literature, the tale has been retold and reimagined by poets such as Ovid and Virgil, and in contemporary works by authors like Neil Gaiman. The theme of love transcending even death resonates deeply, making it a timeless narrative that continues to inspire and move people across generations.

Conclusion

The story of Orpheus and Eurydice is a powerful tale of love, loss, and the consequences of doubt. It highlights the importance of trust and the lengths one will go to for love. Orpheus's journey to the underworld and his tragic failure serve as a poignant reminder of the fragility of happiness and the enduring power of love, even in the face of insurmountable odds.

5.2 PYGMALION AND GALATEA

The myth of Pygmalion and Galatea is a captivating story about love, art, and the power of transformation. It explores the themes of creation, devotion, and the intersection between reality and idealism. Pygmalion, a talented sculptor, falls in love with a statue he carves, and through divine intervention, his beloved creation comes to life.

The Creation of Galatea

Pygmalion was a gifted sculptor from the island of Cyprus. Despite his artistic genius, he was disillusioned with the women of his time, believing them to be flawed and imperfect. Determined to create his vision of the perfect woman, Pygmalion channeled his frustration and longing into his art. He carved a statue out of ivory, painstakingly shaping it into a figure of exquisite beauty. The statue, which he named Galatea, was so lifelike and beautiful that it seemed almost real.

Pygmalion's Love for His Creation

As Pygmalion worked on Galatea, he became increasingly captivated by her beauty. He adorned the statue with fine clothing and precious jewels, treating her as though she were a living woman. Over time, his admiration grew into deep affection, and he found himself in love with his own creation. He would speak to her, caress her, and even kiss her, hoping against hope that she might somehow come to life.

Divine Intervention

Pygmalion's love for Galatea did not go unnoticed by the gods. During the festival of Aphrodite, the goddess of love, Pygmalion prayed fervently at her altar, asking for a wife who would be as perfect as his statue. Touched by his devotion and sincerity, Aphrodite decided to grant his wish. When Pygmalion returned home and kissed Galatea, he felt her lips grow warm and soft. To his astonishment and delight, the statue began to move and breathe. Galatea had come to life.

Galatea's Transformation

Overwhelmed with joy, Pygmalion embraced Galatea, who was now a living, breathing woman. Aphrodite had not only granted life to his creation but had also blessed their union. Pygmalion and Galatea were married and lived happily together, their love a testament to the power of faith and the transformative magic of divine intervention.

Personal Reflections on Pygmalion and Galatea

The story of Pygmalion and Galatea resonates with me as a powerful example of the interplay between creation and love. It reminds me of the passion and dedication that can drive us to achieve our dreams, no matter how impossible they may seem. One personal reflection that comes to mind is the pursuit of creative endeavors. Like Pygmalion, we often pour our hearts and souls into our work, hoping to create something that resonates with others and, in some ways, becomes a part of us.

This myth also speaks to the transformative power of love and belief. Pygmalion's unwavering faith in his vision and his love for Galatea ultimately brought her to life. It serves as a reminder that our deepest desires and sincerest efforts can lead to extraordinary outcomes when we believe in them wholeheartedly.

Cultural Impact and Legacy

The myth of Pygmalion and Galatea has had a significant impact on art, literature, and culture throughout history. The story has been interpreted and reimagined in various forms, from ancient sculptures and paintings to modern plays and films. One of the most famous adaptations is George Bernard Shaw's play "Pygmalion," which was later turned into the beloved musical "My Fair Lady." Shaw's version explores themes of transformation and social class, drawing inspiration from the original myth while addressing contemporary issues.

In addition to its presence in the arts, the story of Pygmalion and Galatea has also influenced psychological concepts, such as the "Pygmalion effect," which describes how high expectations can lead to improved performance and outcomes. This idea underscores the power of belief and the impact of positive reinforcement on human behavior.

Conclusion

The myth of Pygmalion and Galatea is a timeless tale of love, creation, and transformation. It illustrates the profound connection between art and life, and the power of belief to bring dreams to fruition. Pygmalion's devotion to his creation and the divine intervention that brought Galatea to life remind us of the potential for magic and wonder in our own lives. As we continue to explore the myths of love and tragedy, the story of Pygmalion and Galatea stands as a testament to the enduring power of faith, love, and the creative spirit.

The myth of Narcissus and Echo is a poignant tale of unrequited love, vanity, and the consequences of self-obsession. It explores the themes of longing, rejection, and the tragic results of failing to see beyond oneself. Narcissus, a beautiful young man, and Echo, a nymph cursed to only repeat the words of others, are central figures in this timeless story of love and loss.

The Beauty of Narcissus

Narcissus was the son of the river god Cephissus and the nymph Liriope. From a young age, he was renowned for his extraordinary beauty. Everyone who saw him fell in love with him, but Narcissus was indifferent to their admiration and affection. He was so entranced by his own appearance that he could not appreciate the love and attention of others.

Echo's Curse

Echo, a beautiful nymph, was cursed by Hera, the queen of the gods. Hera, suspecting that Echo was helping Zeus to conceal his infidelities, punished her by taking away her ability to speak independently. Echo could only repeat the last words spoken to her, rendering her unable to express her own thoughts and feelings. Despite this, Echo fell deeply in love with Narcissus, drawn to his beauty and charm.

The Meeting of Narcissus and Echo

One day, while wandering through the woods, Narcissus encountered Echo. Unable to speak first, Echo could only follow him and repeat his words. When Narcissus called out, "Who's there?" Echo responded with, "Who's there?" This strange interaction continued until Echo revealed herself to Narcissus. Desperate to express her love, she rushed towards him, but Narcissus cruelly rejected her, telling her to leave him alone. Heartbroken and humiliated, Echo fled into the forest, her love unreturned.

Narcissus's Fate

The goddess Nemesis, who represented divine retribution, witnessed Narcissus's cruelty and decided to punish him for his arrogance and self-absorption. She lured him to a clear pool of water, where he saw his own reflection for the first time. Narcissus was mesmerized by the beauty he saw, not realizing it was his own reflection. He fell hopelessly in love with the image, unable to tear himself away. Consumed by his own reflection, Narcissus pined away and eventually died by the pool, still entranced by his own visage.

The Transformation

After Narcissus's death, the nymphs who mourned him discovered that his body had disappeared. In its place, they found a beautiful flower, which they named the narcissus. This transformation symbolized the enduring nature of his beauty and the tragic consequences of his vanity.

Personal Reflections on Narcissus and Echo

The story of Narcissus and Echo resonates with me because it highlights the dangers of excessive self-love and the pain of unrequited love. One personal reflection that comes to mind is the importance of empathy and understanding in our interactions with others. Narcissus's inability to see beyond his own reflection led to his downfall, reminding us that true beauty and fulfillment come from connecting with and valuing those around us.

Echo's plight also speaks to the struggle of finding one's voice and the pain of being unable to express oneself. Her unrequited love for Narcissus is a powerful reminder of the need for genuine communication and the heartbreak that can result from feeling unheard or dismissed.

Cultural Impact and Legacy

The myth of Narcissus and Echo has left a lasting impact on art, literature, and psychology. The term "narcissism" is derived from Narcissus, describing a personality disorder characterized by excessive self-love and a lack of empathy for others. This concept has become a significant area of study in psychology, reflecting the myth's enduring relevance.

Artists and writers have also been inspired by the tale of Narcissus and Echo. The story has been depicted in paintings, sculptures, and literary works throughout history. For example, the Roman poet Ovid included the myth in his "Metamorphoses," highlighting the themes of transformation and the consequences of vanity.

In modern times, the myth continues to be explored in various forms of media, from literature and film to theater and visual art. Its themes of love, rejection, and self-obsession remain universally relatable, making it a timeless narrative that continues to resonate with audiences.

Conclusion

The myth of Narcissus and Echo is a powerful tale that explores the complexities of love, vanity, and self-awareness. Narcissus's tragic end serves as a cautionary reminder of the dangers of excessive self-love and the importance of empathy and connection with others. Echo's unrequited love and her struggle to find her voice highlight the pain of rejection and the need for genuine communication. As we continue to delve into the myths of love and tragedy, the story of Narcissus and Echo remains a poignant reminder of the consequences of self-obsession and the enduring power of love and connection.

5.4 HADES AND PERSEPHONE

The myth of Hades and Persephone is a captivating tale that explores themes of love, power, and the changing seasons. This story explains the origins of the seasons and highlights the complex relationship between the underworld and the world of the living. Hades, the god of the underworld, and Persephone, the daughter of Demeter, goddess of the harvest, form a union that profoundly impacts both their realms.

The Abduction of Persephone

Persephone, also known as Kore, was the beautiful daughter of Demeter and Zeus. She spent her days frolicking in the meadows, surrounded by flowers and nature. One day, while picking flowers with her friends, Persephone was captivated by a particularly enchanting blossom. As she reached for it, the ground beneath her feet split open, and Hades, the god of the underworld, emerged from the chasm in his chariot. In a swift and sudden act, he abducted Persephone and took her to his dark realm to be his queen.

Demeter's Despair

Demeter, the goddess of the harvest and agriculture, was devastated by the disappearance of her daughter. She searched the earth tirelessly, but Persephone was nowhere to be found. In her grief, Demeter neglected her duties, causing the earth to become barren and lifeless. Crops failed, and famine spread across the land, affecting both mortals and gods. The once-fertile earth turned cold and desolate, reflecting Demeter's sorrow.

The Search and Revelation

As the famine worsened, the cries of the starving reached Olympus, prompting the gods to intervene. Zeus, realizing the gravity of the situation, sent Hermes, the messenger god, to the underworld to negotiate Persephone's release. When Hermes arrived in the underworld, he found Persephone and conveyed Demeter's anguish and the dire state of the earth. Moved by the suffering of both mortals and his own divine kin, Hades agreed to let Persephone return to her mother, but not without a condition.

The Pomegranate Seeds

Before Persephone left the underworld, Hades offered her a pomegranate. Unaware of its significance, she ate six seeds. According to ancient laws, anyone who consumed food or drink in the underworld was bound to it. Thus, by eating the pomegranate seeds, Persephone was compelled to spend part of each year with Hades.

The Cycle of the Seasons

A compromise was reached: Persephone would spend three months of the year in the underworld with Hades and the remaining nine months with her mother, Demeter, on the earth's surface. This arrangement explained the changing seasons. When Persephone was with Hades, Demeter mourned, and the earth experienced winter. When Persephone returned, Demeter rejoiced, bringing spring and summer's warmth and fertility back to the land.

Personal Reflections on Hades and Persephone

The story of Hades and Persephone has always intrigued me because it beautifully intertwines the themes of love, loss, and renewal. One personal reflection that comes to mind is how this myth mirrors the cycles of life and the inevitability of change. Just as Persephone's journey between the underworld and the earth brings about the seasons, our lives are marked by periods of growth, loss, and renewal.

This myth also speaks to the power of resilience and the ability to find balance in the face of adversity. Despite the darkness of the underworld, Persephone adapts to her role as queen, bringing light and life to Hades' realm. Her story reminds us that even in the most challenging circumstances, we can find strength and create harmony.

Cultural Impact and Legacy

The myth of Hades and Persephone has had a profound impact on art, literature, and culture throughout history. Their story has been depicted in ancient Greek pottery, sculptures, and frescoes, illustrating the dramatic abduction and the poignant reunions. Poets such as Ovid and Hesiod have retold the myth, emphasizing different aspects of the tale.

In modern times, the story of Hades and Persephone continues to inspire writers, artists, and filmmakers. It has been adapted into novels, plays, operas, and even graphic novels. For example, the opera "Orpheus and Eurydice" by Christoph Willibald Gluck touches on themes from the myth of Hades and Persephone. Additionally, the graphic novel "Lore Olympus" by Rachel Smythe reimagines their story in a contemporary setting. The themes of love, power, and transformation resonate deeply with audiences, making it a timeless narrative that continues to captivate and inspire.

Conclusion

The myth of Hades and Persephone is a rich and multifaceted tale that explores the complexities of love, power, and the natural world. Their story explains the changing seasons and highlights the balance between light and darkness, life and death. As we continue to delve into the myths of love and tragedy, the tale of Hades and Persephone stands out as a powerful reminder of the cyclical nature of life and the enduring strength of love and resilience.

5.5 PYRAMUS AND THISBE

The myth of Pyramus and Thisbe is a tragic love story that predates and parallels the tale of Romeo and Juliet. It tells of young lovers whose desire to be together is thwarted by their families' animosity and a series of misunderstandings. Their story captures the intensity of youthful passion, the pain of separation, and the devastating consequences of miscommunication.

The Forbidden Love

Pyramus and Thisbe lived in the city of Babylon, in neighboring houses connected by a shared wall. They were considered the most beautiful youth and maiden in the land. As they grew up, they fell deeply in love with each other. However, their families harbored a bitter feud and forbade them from seeing each other or expressing their love openly. Despite their families' enmity, Pyramus and Thisbe communicated through a small crack in the wall that separated their homes. Through this secret passage, they whispered sweet nothings and shared their dreams of being together.

The Secret Meeting

Desperate to be united, Pyramus and Thisbe devised a plan to escape their families' constraints. They decided to meet outside the city, under a mulberry tree near Ninus's tomb, where they could finally be together. As night fell, Thisbe arrived at the rendezvous point first. While waiting for Pyramus, she encountered a lioness with a blood-stained mouth, fresh from a hunt. Terrified, Thisbe fled, leaving behind her veil, which the lioness mauled before disappearing into the woods.

The Tragic Misunderstanding

When Pyramus arrived and found Thisbe's bloodied veil and the tracks of the lioness, he assumed the worst—that his beloved Thisbe had been killed by the beast. Overcome with grief and guilt, Pyramus drew his sword and took his own life, believing that he could not live without Thisbe. His blood splattered on the white berries of the mulberry tree, staining them dark red.

The Heartbreaking Discovery

Shortly after, Thisbe returned to the meeting place, hoping to find Pyramus. Instead, she found his lifeless body beneath the mulberry tree. Devastated by the sight and realizing the tragic misunderstanding, she embraced him and wept. With a broken heart, Thisbe took Pyramus's sword and ended her own life, wishing to join him in death as they could not be together in life.

The Transformation

The gods, moved by the tragic love and devotion of Pyramus and Thisbe, honored their love by turning the mulberry tree's berries from white to the dark red color of their blood. The tree stood as a lasting memorial to the couple's tragic fate and the enduring power of their love.

Personal Reflections on Pyramus and Thisbe

The story of Pyramus and Thisbe resonates deeply with me as a timeless reminder of the power of love and the tragic consequences of miscommunication. One personal reflection that comes to mind is the importance of clear communication and the dangers of making assumptions. The tragic end of Pyramus and Thisbe could have been avoided had they been able to confirm each other's safety and well-being.

Their story also underscores the lengths to which people will go for love and the intense emotions that can drive our actions. The passion and determination of Pyramus and Thisbe to be together, despite their families' feud, highlight the resilience of love and the human spirit's ability to endure in the face of adversity.

Cultural Impact and Legacy

The myth of Pyramus and Thisbe has inspired countless works of art, literature, and theater throughout history. One of the most famous adaptations is William Shakespeare's "Romeo and Juliet," which shares striking similarities with the ancient tale. Shakespeare also included a comedic rendition of the story in "A Midsummer Night's Dream," where a group of amateur actors perform a play based on the myth.

In addition to literature, the story has been depicted in paintings, operas, and modern films, reflecting its enduring appeal and emotional depth. The themes of forbidden love, tragedy, and the consequences of miscommunication continue to resonate with audiences, making it a timeless narrative that speaks to the complexities of human relationships.

Conclusion

The myth of Pyramus and Thisbe is a powerful tale of love, tragedy, and the dire consequences of miscommunication. Their story serves as a poignant reminder of the importance of clear communication and the devastating impact of assumptions. As we continue to explore the myths of love and tragedy, the tale of Pyramus and Thisbe stands as a testament to the enduring power of love and the human desire to overcome obstacles in the pursuit of happiness.

5.6 BAUCIS AND PHILEMON

The myth of Baucis and Philemon is a heartwarming tale of love, hospitality, and divine reward. Unlike many other Greek myths that focus on tragedy and conflict, this story highlights the virtues of kindness and generosity. Baucis and Philemon, an elderly couple, demonstrate that true wealth lies not in material possessions but in the richness of the spirit and the strength of their love.

The Visit of Zeus and Hermes

In ancient Phrygia, a region of modern-day Turkey, lived an elderly couple named Baucis and Philemon. They were poor but deeply devoted to each other and to their simple, pious life. One day, Zeus and Hermes, the king of the gods and the messenger god, decided to visit the earth disguised as mortal travelers. They wanted to test the hospitality of the people in Phrygia.

Disguised as weary travelers, Zeus and Hermes knocked on many doors, asking for food and shelter. However, they were repeatedly turned away by the wealthy and the prosperous, who were too proud or too indifferent to help the strangers.

The Humble Hospitality

Finally, the gods arrived at the humble cottage of Baucis and Philemon. Despite their poverty, the elderly couple welcomed the strangers warmly. They invited them inside, offered them a seat by the fire, and prepared a modest meal. Baucis and Philemon served what little food they had—olives, bread, wine, and vegetables from their garden. They even killed their only goose to provide meat for their guests, though the goose managed to escape.

As the meal progressed, Baucis noticed that the wine jug never emptied, no matter how much they poured. Realizing that their guests were not ordinary mortals, the couple grew fearful and reverent. Zeus and Hermes then revealed their true identities, assuring Baucis and Philemon that their kindness and hospitality had been noted.

The Divine Reward

Impressed by the couple's generosity and piety, Zeus and Hermes led Baucis and Philemon to a nearby hill. From there, the gods revealed their divine powers by flooding the valley below, destroying the homes of the inhospitable people. However, Baucis and Philemon's humble cottage was transformed into a magnificent temple, with golden columns and a marble roof.

As a reward for their kindness, the gods granted Baucis and Philemon a wish. The couple asked to serve as priests in the temple and to die at the same moment, so neither would have to live without the other. Zeus and Hermes granted their wish, and Baucis and Philemon lived the rest of their days serving in the temple.

When their time came, they peacefully transformed into two intertwined trees—an oak and a linden—standing together forever. The trees served as a symbol of their enduring love and the divine favor they had received.

Personal Reflections on Baucis and Philemon

The story of Baucis and Philemon resonates deeply with me because it highlights the virtues of kindness, generosity, and true love. One personal reflection that comes to mind is the importance of hospitality and the impact that small acts of kindness can have. Baucis and Philemon's willingness to share what little they had, despite their poverty, exemplifies the spirit of selflessness and compassion that we should all strive to embody.

Their story also speaks to the power of love and the strength of a lifelong partnership. Baucis and Philemon's request to die together rather than live without each other reflects a deep and enduring bond that transcends the material world. It reminds us that true wealth lies in the relationships we build and the love we share with others.

Cultural Impact and Legacy

The myth of Baucis and Philemon has inspired numerous works of art, literature, and philosophy. The story has been retold by poets such as Ovid in his "Metamorphoses," where it serves as a testament to the values of piety and hospitality. Their tale has been depicted in paintings, sculptures, and even operas, celebrating the virtues of kindness and the rewards of a generous spirit.

In modern times, the story of Baucis and Philemon continues to resonate as a symbol of true love and the importance of treating others with compassion and respect. It serves as a reminder that acts of kindness, no matter how small, can have a profound impact and that love and generosity are the true measures of a person's worth.

Conclusion

The myth of Baucis and Philemon is a beautiful tale that celebrates the virtues of hospitality, generosity, and enduring love. Their story demonstrates that true wealth is not found in material possessions but in the richness of the spirit and the strength of their bond. As we continue to explore the myths of love and tragedy, the tale of Baucis and Philemon stands out as a powerful reminder of the importance of kindness and the lasting rewards of a generous heart.

5.7 SUMMARY AND KEY TAKEAWAYS

Summary

In this chapter, we explored several poignant and powerful myths of love and tragedy, each highlighting different aspects of the human experience and the complexities of relationships.

We began with **Orpheus and Eurydice**, a tale of profound love and the devastating pain of loss. Orpheus's journey to the underworld to retrieve his beloved Eurydice and his ultimate failure due to doubt underscores the fragility of happiness and the importance of trust in love.

Next, we delved into the story of **Pygmalion and Galatea**. Pygmalion, a sculptor who falls in love with his own creation, shows the transformative power of love and belief. The divine intervention that brings Galatea to life highlights the potential for magic and wonder in our lives when we have faith in our dreams.

Narcissus and Echo presented a cautionary tale about vanity and unrequited love. Narcissus's self-obsession and Echo's inability to express her feelings reflect the dangers of excessive self-love and the pain of being unheard.

The myth of **Hades and Persephone** explored the complex relationship between love, power, and the changing seasons. Persephone's abduction by Hades and the resulting compromise between the gods explain the cycle of the seasons and emphasize themes of resilience and adaptation.

Pyramus and Thisbe, a story of forbidden love and tragic misunderstanding, highlighted the intensity of youthful passion and the dire consequences of miscommunication. Their tale serves as a poignant reminder of the importance of clear communication and the devastating impact of assumptions.

Finally, the story of **Baucis and Philemon** celebrated the virtues of hospitality, generosity, and enduring love. Their humble kindness to disguised gods led to their eternal union and transformation into intertwined trees, symbolizing the lasting rewards of a generous heart.

Key Takeaways

Orpheus and Eurydice

- Trust is crucial in relationships, and doubt can lead to tragic outcomes.
- Love can drive us to achieve the impossible, even in the face of great adversity.

Pygmalion and Galatea

- Belief and love have transformative powers.
- The pursuit of creative endeavors can lead to extraordinary outcomes when fueled by passion and faith.

Narcissus and Echo

- Excessive self-love and vanity can lead to isolation and tragedy.
- The pain of unrequited love and the importance of finding one's voice are central themes.

Hades and Persephone

- The myth explains the cycle of the seasons, symbolizing the balance between light and darkness, life and death.
- Resilience and adaptation are key themes in navigating life's changes.

Pyramus and Thisbe

- Miscommunication can have devastating consequences.
- The intensity of youthful love and the willingness to defy societal constraints are highlighted.

Baucis and Philemon

- Hospitality and generosity are virtues that bring divine rewards.
- True wealth lies in the strength of love and the bonds we share with others.

Reflective Questions

- How do the myths in this chapter illustrate the complexities and challenges of love and relationships?
- In what ways do these stories highlight the importance of communication, trust, and empathy in overcoming obstacles?
- How can the virtues of kindness, generosity, and resilience from these myths inspire us in our own lives and relationships?

5.8 MYTHOLOGY QUIZ 5

Test your knowledge about the myths of love and tragedy explored in this chapter with the following questions:

1. **What was the condition Hades set for Orpheus to bring Eurydice back to the living world?**

    A) Orpheus had to defeat Cerberus.

    B) Orpheus had to not look back at Eurydice until they reached the surface.

    C) Orpheus had to bring a golden apple to Hades.

    D) Orpheus had to sing to Hades every night.

2. **What did Pygmalion pray for at the festival of Aphrodite?**

    A) Wealth and prosperity.

    B) Eternal youth.

    C) That his statue would come to life.

    D) A beautiful wife as perfect as his statue.

3. **Why was Echo unable to express her own thoughts and feelings?**

    A) She had taken a vow of silence.

    B) She was cursed by Hera to only repeat the words of others.

    C) She was born mute.

    D) She was enchanted by a sorcerer.

4. **How did Narcissus die?**

    A) He was killed by a rival.

    B) He drowned while looking at his reflection.

    C) He was cursed by the gods.

    D) He starved to death, entranced by his own reflection.

5. **What did Persephone eat that bound her to the underworld for part of the year?**

    A) A pomegranate.

    B) An apple.

    C) A grape.

    D) A fig.

6. **How did Pyramus and Thisbe communicate despite their families' feud?**

    A) Through secret letters.

    B) By meeting in a hidden cave.

    C) Through a crack in the wall between their houses.

    D) By sending messages through a servant.

7. **What transformation did Baucis and Philemon undergo as a reward for their hospitality?**

    A) They became gods.

    B) They were turned into golden statues.

C) They were transformed into intertwined trees.

D) They received eternal youth.

Note: Answers to the quiz can be found in the "Answer Key" section in the Appendix.

CHAPTER 6:
THE UNDERWORLD AND AFTERLIFE

6.1 THE REALM OF HADES

The ancient Greeks believed that the underworld, known as the Realm of Hades, was the final destination for the souls of the dead. Governed by Hades, the god of the underworld, this shadowy realm was a place where the souls of the departed would go to their eternal rest or punishment. Understanding the Realm of Hades gives us insight into the Greek conception of life after death and the moral structure of their mythology.

Hades, the God of the Underworld

Hades, also known as Pluto, was one of the three brothers who divided the world among themselves after overthrowing the Titans. While Zeus took the sky and Poseidon the sea, Hades was given dominion over the underworld. Unlike his brothers, Hades rarely left his dark kingdom, ruling over the dead with a stern but fair hand. He was not evil, as often misconstrued, but rather a just ruler who ensured that the deceased received their due.

The Geography of the Underworld

The underworld was a complex and multi-layered place with several distinct regions, each serving different purposes and housing different souls. The entrance to the underworld was often depicted as a dark cave or a deep chasm, guarded by Cerberus, the ferocious three-headed dog. Cerberus allowed the dead to enter but prevented them from leaving.

Key Regions of the Underworld

- **Asphodel Meadows**: This region was the dwelling place for ordinary souls who had lived neither particularly virtuous nor particularly wicked lives. The Asphodel Meadows were a vast, gray expanse where the souls of the dead wandered aimlessly, living out a monotonous existence without pleasure or pain.
- **Elysian Fields (Elysium)**: Elysium was the paradisiacal part of the underworld, reserved for heroes, the righteous, and those favored by the gods. It was a place of eternal springtime, where the souls enjoyed a blissful afterlife, indulging in whatever pleasures they had known in life. The Elysian Fields represented the ultimate reward for a life well-lived.
- **Tartarus**: Tartarus was the deepest, darkest part of the underworld, a place of eternal torment for the wicked and the enemies of the gods. Titans and other monstrous beings were imprisoned here, along with mortals who had committed

grievous sins. Tartarus was a place of suffering and punishment, designed to keep its inhabitants in perpetual agony.

Judgment in the Underworld

Upon arrival in the underworld, souls were judged by three judges: Minos, Rhadamanthus, and Aeacus. These judges determined the fate of each soul, directing them to the Asphodel Meadows, Elysium, or Tartarus based on their deeds in life. This process underscored the Greek belief in justice and the idea that one's actions in life would determine their fate in the afterlife.

The Role of Hades and Persephone

Hades ruled the underworld with his queen, Persephone, whom he had abducted and made his wife. Persephone's presence brought a measure of compassion and change to the otherwise static realm. Together, they maintained the balance of the underworld, ensuring that the cycle of life and death continued unbroken.

Personal Reflections on the Realm of Hades

The concept of the Realm of Hades offers a fascinating glimpse into how the ancient Greeks understood life, death, and morality. One personal reflection that comes to mind is the importance of living a balanced life. The idea that our actions have consequences in the afterlife serves as a reminder to strive for virtue and justice in our daily lives.

This mythological view also highlights the Greek understanding of the duality of existence—light and dark, joy and suffering. The underworld was not merely a place of punishment but also a realm where the soul's true nature and life's deeds were reflected and judged.

Cultural Impact and Legacy

The Realm of Hades has had a profound influence on Western culture and literature. Its depiction in ancient texts, such as Homer's "Odyssey" and Virgil's "Aeneid," has shaped the way we think about the afterlife and the moral implications of our actions. The underworld continues to be a rich source of inspiration for writers, artists, and filmmakers, symbolizing the ultimate journey that every soul must undertake.

In modern culture, the underworld is often portrayed in books, movies, and television series, reinforcing the enduring legacy of Greek mythology. For instance, the TV series "Lucifer" explores themes of life, death, and the afterlife, drawing inspiration from various mythologies, including Greek. These stories continue to explore themes of life, death, and the afterlife, reminding us of the timeless human quest to understand what lies beyond our mortal existence.

Conclusion

The Realm of Hades is a complex and multifaceted part of Greek mythology, representing the ultimate destination for souls after death. Governed by Hades and Persephone, it encompasses regions of reward, punishment, and mundane existence, reflecting the moral and ethical beliefs of ancient Greece. As we delve deeper into the myths of the underworld, the story of Hades and his realm offers profound insights into the Greek understanding of life, death, and the afterlife.

6.2 THE RIVER STYX

The River Styx is one of the most significant and iconic elements in Greek mythology, symbolizing the boundary between the world of the living and the realm of the dead. Its name, meaning "hateful" or "abhorred," reflects the fear and reverence with which the ancient Greeks regarded this mythical river. The River Styx is more than just a physical boundary; it is a crucial component of the mythological landscape, representing oaths, transformation, and the immutable separation between life and death.

The Importance of the River Styx

The River Styx flowed through the underworld and encircled it nine times, creating a formidable barrier that souls had to cross to reach their final destination. It was considered the principal river of the underworld, and its waters were imbued with magical properties. According to myth, the gods themselves would swear oaths by the Styx, as it was deemed the most sacred and binding of all vows. Breaking an oath sworn on the Styx would result in severe punishment, even for the gods.

The Role of Charon, the Ferryman

Charon, the aged and grim ferryman of the underworld, played a vital role in transporting souls across the River Styx. For a small fee, usually a coin placed in the mouth of the deceased, Charon would ferry the souls of the dead to the other side. Those who could not pay the fare were doomed to wander the banks of the Styx for a hundred years, unable to reach their final resting place.

Charon's role highlights the ancient Greek practices surrounding death and burial. Proper funeral rites, including the placement of a coin for Charon's fee, were essential to ensure the soul's safe passage to the underworld. This tradition underscored the importance of honoring the dead and the belief in an afterlife where the soul's journey continued.

The Waters of the Styx

The waters of the River Styx were believed to possess extraordinary and often deadly properties. According to myth, the river's waters could confer invulnerability or bring about death. One of the most famous tales involving the Styx's waters is that of Achilles. His mother, Thetis, dipped him into the River Styx as an infant, making him invulnerable except for the heel by which she held him—the origin of the term "Achilles' heel."

The magical properties of the Styx also extended to its use as a powerful poison. The river's water was said to be so potent that it could kill gods and mortals alike. This dual nature of the Styx, as both a protective and destructive force, highlights the river's complexity and significance in Greek mythology.

The Symbolism of the River Styx

The River Styx symbolizes the ultimate boundary between life and death, a crossing that every soul must undertake. It represents the transition from the known world to the unknown, from the mortal realm to the eternal afterlife. Styx's role in oath-taking among the gods further emphasizes its importance as a symbol of unbreakable promises and the seriousness with which such vows were regarded.

The river also embodies the themes of transformation and purification. Just as the souls of the dead must cross the Styx to reach their final destination, the river itself serves as a metaphor for the journey of the soul and the trials it must endure to achieve rest or retribution.

Personal Reflections on the River Styx

The story of the River Styx resonates with me as a powerful symbol of boundaries and transitions. One personal reflection that comes to mind is the idea of crossing significant thresholds in life, whether they be emotional, physical, or spiritual. Just as the souls of the dead must cross the Styx to reach the underworld, we too encounter moments in life where we must move from one phase to another, often facing uncertainty and change.

This myth also speaks to the importance of honoring commitments and the weight of our promises. The gods' reverence for oaths sworn on the Styx reminds us that our words and actions carry significant consequences, and we should approach them with the same seriousness and integrity.

Cultural Impact and Legacy

The River Styx has left an indelible mark on Western culture and literature. Its imagery and symbolism have been depicted in countless works of art, from ancient Greek pottery and sculptures to modern paintings and films. The concept of a river that separates the living from the dead is a recurring motif in many cultures, reflecting a universal human fascination with the afterlife and the mysteries that lie beyond.

In contemporary literature and media, the River Styx continues to serve as a powerful symbol. It appears in novels, movies, and television series, often depicted as a foreboding and mystical barrier that characters must cross to reach the underworld. For instance, in the "Percy Jackson & the Olympians" series by Rick Riordan, the River Styx is portrayed as a perilous boundary that heroes must navigate. This imagery reinforces the idea of the Styx as a gateway to the unknown and a place of transformation.

Conclusion

The River Styx is a central element of Greek mythology, symbolizing the boundary between life and death, and the transition from the mortal world to the afterlife. It represents themes of transformation, purification, and the weight of oaths and commitments. As we explore the myths surrounding the underworld and afterlife, the story of the River Styx reminds us of the profound and universal human desire to understand and navigate the mysteries of existence.

6.3 THE ELYSIAN FIELDS

The Elysian Fields, also known as Elysium, are one of the most idyllic and serene parts of the Greek underworld. Reserved for the souls of heroes, the righteous, and those favored by the gods, the Elysian Fields represent the ultimate paradise where the dead can enjoy eternal peace and happiness. This concept of a blissful afterlife reflects the ancient Greeks' beliefs about reward, virtue, and the possibility of a happy existence beyond death.

The Nature of the Elysian Fields

The Elysian Fields are depicted as a place of eternal springtime, bathed in warm sunlight and filled with lush meadows, blooming flowers, and gentle streams. Unlike other parts of the underworld, which are often dark and foreboding, Elysium is a realm of beauty and tranquility. The souls who reside here experience no pain, sorrow, or suffering. Instead, they enjoy endless leisure, engaging in the activities they loved during their lifetimes, such as music, dance, and feasting.

Inhabitants of Elysium

Elysium is reserved for those who have lived virtuous lives, performed heroic deeds, or earned the favor of the gods. This includes legendary heroes like Achilles, who was brought to Elysium by his divine mother Thetis, and other mortals who distinguished themselves through their actions and character. Poets, philosophers, and other individuals who made significant contributions to society were also believed to inhabit Elysium, enjoying the rewards of their virtuous lives.

The Path to Elysium

Reaching Elysium was not guaranteed for every soul. The journey to the Elysian Fields began with the judgment of the dead, overseen by Minos, Rhadamanthus, and Aeacus. These judges evaluated the deeds of each soul, determining whether they were worthy of entering Elysium, destined for the Asphodel Meadows, or condemned to Tartarus. Those deemed worthy were granted entry into Elysium, where they could spend eternity in bliss.

Elysium in Mythology

The concept of Elysium appears in various works of ancient literature, including Homer's "Odyssey" and Hesiod's "Works and Days." In the "Odyssey," Menelaus is told that he will be sent to Elysium instead of dying in the usual manner, as a reward for being the husband of Helen and the son-in-law of Zeus. Hesiod describes Elysium as the Isle of the Blessed, a place where the favored of the gods live a life of ease and pleasure.

The Roman poet Virgil also described Elysium in his epic "Aeneid." In this work, the hero Aeneas visits the underworld and sees Elysium, where the souls of the blessed dwell. Virgil's depiction emphasizes the beauty and tranquility of Elysium, reinforcing its status as the ultimate reward for a life well-lived.

Personal Reflections on the Elysian Fields

The idea of the Elysian Fields resonates with me as a symbol of hope and the possibility of reward for a virtuous life. One personal reflection that comes to mind is the importance of striving to live a life of integrity and kindness. The promise of Elysium encourages us to pursue goodness and excellence, not just for the potential rewards in the afterlife, but for the positive impact it has on our lives and the lives of others.

This myth also speaks to the human desire for happiness and peace. The Elysian Fields represent the fulfillment of our deepest aspirations for a place where we can find rest and joy after the struggles of life. It reminds us of the value of creating moments of beauty and tranquility in our everyday lives.

Cultural Impact and Legacy

The concept of the Elysian Fields has had a profound impact on Western thought and culture. It has influenced various religious and philosophical ideas about the afterlife, including the Christian notion of heaven as a place of eternal peace and joy. The imagery of Elysium has been depicted in countless works of art, literature, and music, from classical antiquity to the modern era.

In contemporary culture, the idea of a paradise-like afterlife continues to inspire artists and storytellers. The Elysian Fields appear in films, books, and television series as a symbol of ultimate reward and happiness. For instance, the Elysian Fields are depicted in the movie "Gladiator," where the protagonist Maximus envisions reuniting with his family in this idyllic afterlife. This enduring legacy reflects the universal human longing for a better world beyond this one.

Conclusion

The Elysian Fields, with their serene beauty and promise of eternal happiness, represent the pinnacle of reward in Greek mythology. Reserved for the virtuous and the heroic, Elysium embodies the hope for a peaceful and joyous afterlife. As we explore the myths of the underworld and afterlife, the story of the Elysian Fields offers a powerful reminder of the importance of living a life of virtue and the timeless human quest for paradise.

6.4 TARTARUS AND PUNISHMENT

Tartarus is one of the most feared and dreaded parts of the Greek underworld. Unlike the serene and blissful Elysian Fields, Tartarus is a place of darkness, torment, and eternal punishment. Reserved for the wicked, the monstrous, and the enemies of the gods, Tartarus serves as the ultimate prison for those who have committed grievous sins. Its depiction in Greek mythology highlights themes of justice, retribution, and the moral order of the cosmos.

The Nature of Tartarus

Tartarus is located deep beneath the underworld, even below the Asphodel Meadows and the Elysian Fields. It is described as a dark, gloomy abyss, surrounded by impenetrable walls and guarded by formidable gates. The Greek poet Hesiod, in his "Theogony," described Tartarus as being as far beneath the earth as the earth is beneath the sky. This immense depth emphasizes the remoteness and inaccessibility of Tartarus, reinforcing its role as a place of extreme punishment.

Inhabitants of Tartarus

The inhabitants of Tartarus are those who have committed the most egregious offenses against the gods and humanity. This includes both mortals and immortals who have defied the divine order. Some of the most famous figures condemned to Tartarus include:

1. **The Titans**: After the Titanomachy, the great war between the Titans and the Olympian gods, the defeated Titans were cast into Tartarus as punishment. They were imprisoned there, bound in chains and subjected to eternal torment for their rebellion against Zeus and the Olympian order.
2. **Sisyphus**: King Sisyphus was condemned to Tartarus for his deceitful and treacherous behavior. His punishment was to roll a massive boulder up a hill, only for it to roll back down

each time he neared the summit. This futile and unending task symbolizes the consequences of hubris and the futility of attempting to outsmart the gods.

3. **Tantalus**: Tantalus, a mortal king, was punished in Tartarus for his heinous crimes, which included stealing ambrosia from the gods and attempting to serve his own son as a meal to the Olympians. His punishment was to stand in a pool of water beneath a fruit tree, forever tormented by thirst and hunger. Each time he reached for the water or fruit, they would recede out of reach, leaving him in eternal suffering.

4. **Ixion**: Ixion was punished for his audacity in attempting to seduce Hera, the wife of Zeus. His eternal punishment was to be bound to a fiery, spinning wheel, continuously turning without end. This gruesome fate reflects the severe consequences of betraying the trust of the gods.

The Role of Tartarus in Mythology

Tartarus serves as a symbol of divine justice and retribution. It represents the moral order of the universe, where those who commit grave sins and offenses are held accountable for their actions. The torments of Tartarus are tailored to the crimes of the condemned, emphasizing the idea that punishment should fit the offense.

The presence of Tartarus in Greek mythology reinforces the belief that the gods are not only powerful but also just. It serves as a deterrent to those who might consider defying the divine order or committing acts of wickedness. The stories of those condemned to Tartarus remind mortals and immortals alike of the consequences of their actions and the importance of adhering to moral and ethical principles.

Personal Reflections on Tartarus

The concept of Tartarus resonates with me as a stark reminder of the importance of justice and accountability. One personal reflection that comes to mind is the idea that our actions have consequences, and we must strive to live with integrity and respect for others. The stories of Sisyphus, Tantalus, and other inhabitants of Tartarus illustrate the severe repercussions of deceit, betrayal, and hubris.

This myth also speaks to the human desire for justice and the belief in a moral order that holds individuals accountable for their actions. Tartarus serves as a powerful symbol of retribution and the idea that no one, not even the most powerful, is above the law.

Cultural Impact and Legacy

The imagery and themes of Tartarus have left a lasting impact on Western culture and literature. The concept of a place of punishment for the wicked has influenced various religious and philosophical ideas about the afterlife, including the Christian notion of hell. Tartarus has been depicted in numerous works of art, literature, and music, from classical antiquity to the modern era.

In contemporary culture, the idea of Tartarus continues to inspire storytellers and artists. It appears in novels, films, and television series as a symbol of ultimate punishment and retribution. For instance, in the novel "The House of Hades" by Rick Riordan, Tartarus is depicted as a terrifying and inescapable realm of suffering. The enduring legacy of Tartarus reflects the universal human fascination with justice and the consequences of one's actions.

Conclusion

Tartarus is a central element of Greek mythology, representing the ultimate destination for those who have committed the most grievous sins. As a place of darkness, torment, and eternal punishment, it serves as a powerful symbol of divine justice and retribution. The stories of those condemned to Tartarus remind us of the importance of living with integrity and respect for the moral order of the universe. As we continue to explore the myths of the underworld and afterlife, the tale of Tartarus offers profound insights into the ancient Greek understanding of justice and the consequences of wickedness.

6.5 THE STORY OF SISYPHUS

The story of Sisyphus is one of the most famous and enduring myths in Greek mythology, symbolizing the futile and repetitive nature of certain human endeavors. Sisyphus, a king known for his cunning and deceit, was condemned to an eternal punishment that has come to represent the ultimate expression of futility and endless toil. This myth explores themes of hubris, punishment, and the human condition.

The Life and Deeds of Sisyphus

Sisyphus was the king of Ephyra (later known as Corinth), renowned for his cleverness and trickery. He was the son of Aeolus, the ruler of Thessaly, and Enarete. Despite his noble lineage, Sisyphus became infamous for his deceitful and treacherous behavior. He often used his wit and guile to outsmart others, including the gods.

Deceiving the Gods

One of Sisyphus's most notable acts of deception involved tricking the god of death, Thanatos. Zeus, angered by Sisyphus's constant trickery and defiance of the gods, ordered Thanatos to chain Sisyphus and take him to the underworld. However, Sisyphus managed to outsmart Thanatos by asking him to demonstrate how the chains worked. When Thanatos obliged, Sisyphus quickly chained the god instead, effectively preventing death from taking any mortals. As a result, no one on earth could die, causing chaos and anger among the gods.

Eventually, Ares, the god of war, intervened and freed Thanatos, ensuring the natural order was restored. Sisyphus was then taken to the underworld, but his cunning was not yet exhausted.

Tricking Hades

In the underworld, Sisyphus continued his deceitful ways. Before his death, he had instructed his wife, Merope, not to perform the proper burial rites for him. Upon arriving in the underworld, Sisyphus complained to Hades about his improper burial and persuaded the god to allow him to return to the living world to rectify the situation. Once back on earth, Sisyphus refused to return to the underworld, enjoying his extended life and freedom.

The Eternal Punishment

Zeus, furious with Sisyphus's repeated defiance and trickery, finally decided to impose a punishment that the cunning king could never escape. Sisyphus was condemned to an eternity of rolling a massive boulder up a steep hill. Each time he neared the summit, the boulder would roll back down, forcing Sisyphus to begin the task anew. This endless, futile labor became a powerful symbol of pointless effort and eternal frustration.

Symbolism of the Myth

The story of Sisyphus is rich with symbolism, particularly in its depiction of futile labor and the human struggle for meaning. Sisyphus's punishment represents the endless and often fruitless efforts that can characterize human existence. Despite his cleverness and resourcefulness, Sisyphus is ultimately trapped in a cycle of meaningless toil, reflecting the existential challenges faced by humanity.

The myth also serves as a cautionary tale about hubris and the consequences of defying the natural order. Sisyphus's repeated attempts to outsmart the gods and cheat death highlight the dangers of excessive pride and the inevitable retribution that follows.

Personal Reflections on the Story of Sisyphus

The story of Sisyphus resonates with me as a powerful metaphor for the challenges and struggles we encounter in life. One personal reflection that comes to mind is the idea of perseverance in the face of seemingly insurmountable obstacles. While Sisyphus's task is ultimately futile, his determination to continue pushing the boulder up the hill, despite the inevitability of failure, speaks to the resilience and tenacity of the human spirit.

This myth also prompts me to consider the importance of finding meaning and purpose in our endeavors. Sisyphus's endless toil can serve as a reminder to seek fulfillment in our actions and to strive for goals that bring genuine satisfaction and value to our lives.

Cultural Impact and Legacy

The story of Sisyphus has had a profound impact on literature, philosophy, and popular culture. The existential philosopher Albert Camus famously used the myth as a central metaphor in his essay "The Myth of Sisyphus," exploring the absurdity of human existence and the search for meaning in a seemingly indifferent universe. Camus argued that Sisyphus's defiance in the face of his eternal punishment embodies the human struggle to find purpose and dignity despite the inevitability of suffering.

In addition to its philosophical implications, the myth of Sisyphus has been depicted in various forms of art, literature, and media. It continues to inspire modern interpretations, reflecting the timeless nature of its themes and its relevance to the human condition.

Conclusion

The story of Sisyphus is a compelling and thought-provoking myth that explores themes of hubris, punishment, and the human struggle for meaning. Sisyphus's eternal punishment serves as a powerful symbol of futile labor and the resilience of the human spirit. As we delve deeper into the myths of the underworld and afterlife, the tale of Sisyphus offers valuable insights into the complexities of the human experience and the timeless quest for purpose and understanding.

6.6 THE PUNISHMENT OF TANTALUS

The story of Tantalus is another poignant tale from Greek mythology that explores themes of hubris, divine retribution, and eternal punishment. Tantalus, a mortal king who committed grave offenses against the gods, was condemned to suffer a uniquely tormenting punishment in the underworld. His tale serves as a powerful reminder of the consequences of offending the divine and the perpetual nature of some forms of suffering.

The Crimes of Tantalus

Tantalus was the son of Zeus and the nymph Plouto, making him a favored mortal with divine connections. He was the king of Sipylus, a wealthy and powerful ruler who had the privilege of dining with the gods on Mount Olympus. However, Tantalus's privileged position led him to commit several grievous acts that would seal his fate.

One of Tantalus's most infamous crimes was stealing ambrosia and nectar, the food and drink of the gods, and sharing it with mortals. This act of theft was seen as a serious violation of divine law, as ambrosia and nectar were considered sacred and exclusive to the gods.

However, the most heinous crime committed by Tantalus was the murder of his own son, Pelops. Seeking to test the omniscience of the gods or perhaps out of sheer malice, Tantalus killed Pelops, cooked his body, and served it to the gods at a banquet. The gods, realizing the horrific nature of the meal, refused to partake. They were deeply outraged by Tantalus's abhorrent act and restored Pelops to life, whole and unharmed.

The Eternal Punishment

For his crimes, Tantalus was condemned to Tartarus, the deepest part of the underworld reserved for the most egregious offenders. His punishment was to stand in a pool of water beneath a fruit tree with low branches. Whenever Tantalus reached for the fruit, the branches would lift out of his grasp. When he bent down to drink the water, it would recede, leaving him perpetually thirsty and hungry. This eternal torment gave rise to the term "tantalize," meaning to tease or torment with the promise of something unattainable.

Symbolism of the Punishment

Tantalus's punishment is rich with symbolic meaning. It represents the consequences of hubris and the violation of divine law. By attempting to deceive the gods and commit an unspeakable act of sacrilege, Tantalus doomed himself to a fate of eternal longing and unfulfilled desire. His torment underscores the importance of respecting the boundaries between mortals and the divine.

The nature of Tantalus's punishment—being perpetually close to sustenance yet never able to attain it—highlights the futility and despair that can result from overreaching ambition and moral transgression. It serves as a powerful metaphor for the insatiable desires that can lead to one's downfall.

Personal Reflections on the Punishment of Tantalus

The story of Tantalus resonates with me as a cautionary tale about the dangers of hubris and the consequences of immoral actions. One personal reflection that comes to mind is the importance of humility and respect for the natural and moral order. Tantalus's desire to challenge the gods and break sacred laws ultimately led to his eternal suffering, reminding us that our actions have far-reaching consequences.

This myth also speaks to the human experience of unfulfilled desires and the torment of being close to achieving something yet never quite reaching it. Tantalus's punishment serves as a poignant reminder of the importance of contentment and the dangers of excessive ambition.

Cultural Impact and Legacy

The punishment of Tantalus has left a lasting impact on Western culture and language. The term "tantalize" directly stems from Tantalus's torment and is commonly used to describe situations where someone is teased with the promise of something desirable but unattainable. The story has been depicted in various works of art, literature, and music, illustrating the timeless nature of its themes.

In literature, the tale of Tantalus has been explored by poets such as Ovid and Dante, who included references to Tantalus in their works. In Dante's "Inferno," Tantalus is mentioned as one of the souls suffering in the underworld, highlighting the enduring legacy of his story.

Conclusion

The punishment of Tantalus is a powerful and enduring myth that explores themes of hubris, divine retribution, and eternal suffering. His tale serves as a stark reminder of the consequences of violating sacred laws and challenging the divine order. As we continue to delve into the myths of the underworld and afterlife, the story of Tantalus offers valuable insights into the moral and ethical beliefs of ancient Greece and the timeless lessons they impart.

6.7 SUMMARY AND KEY TAKEAWAYS

Summary

In this chapter, we delved into the dark and enigmatic realms of the Greek underworld, exploring various aspects of life after death as envisioned by ancient Greek mythology. Each section offered a detailed look into different regions and figures within the underworld, highlighting their roles and significance.

We began with **The Realm of Hades**, the overall domain of the god Hades, who ruled over the dead. This section described the geography and structure of the underworld, emphasizing the different areas where souls resided based on their earthly deeds.

Next, we explored **The River Styx**, a crucial boundary within the underworld, symbolizing the separation between life and death. The river's sacred waters and the role of Charon, the ferryman, illustrated the process by which souls crossed into the afterlife.

In **The Elysian Fields**, we learned about the idyllic paradise reserved for heroes and the righteous. This realm of eternal bliss represents the ultimate reward for a virtuous life and contrasts sharply with other parts of the underworld.

Tartarus and Punishment took us to the darkest depths of the underworld, where the wicked and the enemies of the gods faced eternal torment. This section highlighted the severe retributions meted out to those who defied divine law.

The **Story of Sisyphus** provided a poignant example of eternal punishment. Sisyphus's endless task of rolling a boulder up a hill only to have it roll back down symbolizes the futility and despair of defying the gods.

Finally, we examined **The Punishment of Tantalus**, another tale of eternal suffering. Tantalus's unending torment of hunger and thirst, despite being close to sustenance, reflects the dire consequences of his sacrilegious actions.

Key Takeaways

The Realm of Hades

- The underworld is a complex and multi-layered domain where souls are judged and sent to different regions based on their earthly deeds.
- Hades, the god of the underworld, rules this realm with fairness, ensuring that the deceased receive their due rewards or punishments.

The River Styx

- The River Styx serves as the boundary between the living and the dead, symbolizing the final transition into the afterlife.
- Charon, the ferryman, plays a crucial role in transporting souls across the river, underscoring the importance of proper burial rites.

The Elysian Fields

- The Elysian Fields represent the ultimate paradise for heroes and the righteous, offering eternal happiness and peace.
- This concept emphasizes the ancient Greek belief in reward for virtue and heroism.

Tartarus and Punishment

- Tartarus is the deepest part of the underworld, reserved for the most egregious sinners and enemies of the gods.
- The severe punishments in Tartarus highlight the moral order and justice upheld by the gods.

The Story of Sisyphus

- Sisyphus's endless and futile task symbolizes the consequences of hubris and deceit against the gods.
- His story serves as a reminder of the importance of humility and the inevitability of divine retribution.

The Punishment of Tantalus

- Tantalus's eternal torment of unreachable sustenance reflects the severe repercussions of his sacrilegious actions.
- His tale underscores the importance of respecting divine boundaries and the dire consequences of violating them.

Reflective Questions

- How do the different regions of the underworld reflect the ancient Greek views on justice and morality?
- In what ways do the stories of Sisyphus and Tantalus illustrate the consequences of defying the gods and the importance of humility?
- How can the concept of the Elysian Fields inspire us to strive for virtue and heroism in our own lives?

6.8 MYTHOLOGY QUIZ 6

Test your knowledge about the Greek underworld and its fascinating myths with the following questions:

1. **Who is the ruler of the underworld in Greek mythology?**

    A) Zeus

    B) Poseidon

    C) Hades

    D) Ares

2. **What is the River Styx known for in Greek mythology?**

    A) The source of all life

    B) The boundary between the living and the dead

    C) The river of healing

    D) The river of wisdom

3. **Who ferries souls across the River Styx?**

    A) Hermes

    B) Cerberus

    C) Charon

    D) Persephone

4. **What is the Elysian Fields a symbol of?**

    A) Eternal punishment

    B) Eternal bliss and paradise

    C) Eternal struggle

    D) Eternal darkness

5. **Which region of the underworld is reserved for the wicked and the enemies of the gods?**

    A) Elysium

    B) Asphodel Meadows

    C) Tartarus

    D) The River Styx

6. **What was Sisyphus's punishment in the underworld?**

    A) Being chained to a rock

    B) Rolling a boulder up a hill, only for it to roll back down each time

    C) Being turned into a tree

    D) Standing in a pool of water he could never drink from

7. **Why was Tantalus punished in the underworld?**

    A) For stealing fire from the gods

    B) For attempting to seduce Hera

C) For murdering his son and serving him to the gods

D) For blasphemy against Athena

8. **What was Tantalus's punishment in Tartarus?**

A) Being chained to a rock

B) Pushing a boulder up a hill

C) Standing in a pool of water under a fruit tree, forever unable to drink or eat

D) Endlessly spinning on a fiery wheel

Note: Answers to the quiz can be found in the "Answer Key" section in the Appendix.

CHAPTER 7:
THE INFLUENCE OF GREEK MYTHOLOGY

7.1 MYTHOLOGY IN ANCIENT GREEK CULTURE

Greek mythology is not just a collection of ancient stories; it was a central part of everyday life in ancient Greece. These myths were woven into the fabric of Greek culture, influencing everything from religious practices to social norms, and even the arts and sciences.

Understanding how mythology permeated ancient Greek culture helps us appreciate its enduring legacy.

Daily Life and Religious Practices

In ancient Greece, mythology played a vital role in religion. The Greeks believed that gods and goddesses interacted with the mortal world and influenced their lives. Temples dedicated to deities like Zeus, Athena, and Apollo were central to community life. These sacred places were sites of worship, where people offered prayers and sacrifices to seek divine favor or guidance.

Festivals were another important aspect of religious life, often linked to myths. For example, the Panathenaic Festival in Athens honored Athena, the city's patron goddess. During these festivals, myths were retold through plays, songs, and ceremonies, reinforcing communal bonds and shared beliefs.

Education and Morality

Greek mythology was also a cornerstone of education. Stories of gods, heroes, and monsters were used to teach moral lessons and cultural values. Children learned about bravery, loyalty, and the consequences of hubris through tales of Heracles, Achilles, and other legendary figures. These myths served as both entertainment and instruction, shaping the ethical framework of society.

Philosophers like Plato and Aristotle engaged with mythology, sometimes critically, to explore philosophical ideas. For instance, Plato's dialogues often reference myths to illustrate deeper truths about human nature and the cosmos. Myths provided a common language through which complex concepts could be communicated.

Art and Architecture

The influence of mythology on Greek art and architecture is profound. Artists drew inspiration from mythological themes to create sculptures, pottery, and paintings. The Parthenon, one of the most famous architectural achievements of ancient Greece, is adorned with sculptures depicting scenes from myths, such as the birth of Athena and the battle between the gods and giants.

Pottery, a common household item, often featured intricate designs illustrating popular myths. These images served not only as decoration but also as reminders of the stories and their moral lessons. The beauty and skill evident in these works reflect the importance of mythology in Greek artistic expression.

Literature and Theater

Greek mythology was a rich source of material for writers and playwrights. Epic poems like Homer's "Iliad" and "Odyssey" are foundational texts of Western literature, filled with mythological characters and themes. These works not only entertained but also conveyed the values and ideals of Greek society.

In theater, playwrights like Aeschylus, Sophocles, and Euripides brought myths to life on stage. Tragedies such as "Oedipus Rex" and "Medea" explored human emotions and moral dilemmas, often drawing on well-known myths to create powerful narratives. Theater was a communal activity, where citizens gathered to reflect on their shared heritage and societal issues.

Mythology in Social Norms

Myths also influenced social norms and practices. The stories of gods and heroes set standards for behavior and provided models for personal conduct. For example, the concept of xenia, or hospitality, was exemplified in myths like that of Baucis and Philemon, who were rewarded by the gods for their kindness to strangers.

Gender roles were often reinforced through mythological narratives. Goddesses like Hera and Demeter represented ideals of marriage and motherhood, while Artemis symbolized independence and chastity. These stories helped to define and justify societal expectations for men and women.

Personal Reflections on Mythology in Ancient Greek Culture

Reflecting on the role of mythology in ancient Greek culture, it's fascinating to see how deeply these stories were embedded in every aspect of life. One personal reflection that comes to mind is the power of storytelling in shaping cultural identity and values. The myths provided a common framework through which people could understand their world and their place within it.

This integration of mythology into daily life also highlights the importance of shared narratives in building community and continuity. The retelling of myths through festivals, art, and literature ensured that these stories were passed down through generations, preserving the cultural heritage of ancient Greece.

Cultural Impact and Legacy

The influence of Greek mythology extends far beyond ancient Greece. Its themes and characters have permeated Western culture, inspiring countless works of art, literature, and philosophy. Modern adaptations of Greek myths continue to captivate audiences, demonstrating the timeless appeal of these ancient stories.

Greek mythology has also contributed to the development of the humanities and social sciences. The study of myths provides insights into the human psyche, societal norms, and cultural evolution. The enduring legacy of Greek mythology is a testament to its profound impact on human thought and creativity.

Conclusion

Mythology was an integral part of ancient Greek culture, influencing religion, education, art, literature, and social norms. The stories of gods, heroes, and monsters provided a rich tapestry of narratives that shaped every aspect of Greek life. As we explore the legacy of Greek myths, we gain a deeper understanding of the values and beliefs that continue to resonate through history. The myths of ancient Greece remind us of the enduring power of storytelling to connect, educate, and inspire.

7.2 THE LEGACY OF GREEK MYTHS IN ART AND LITERATURE

Greek mythology has left an indelible mark on art and literature throughout history, shaping the creative expressions of countless cultures and eras. The myths of ancient Greece, with their rich narratives and complex characters, have provided a fertile source of inspiration for artists and writers from antiquity to the modern day. Understanding this legacy helps us appreciate the enduring influence of these ancient stories on our own cultural landscape.

Ancient Art and Literature

From the moment they were first told, Greek myths captivated the imaginations of artists and writers in the ancient world. These stories were brought to life in various forms, from epic poetry and drama to sculpture and pottery.

Epic Poetry and Drama

The epic poems of Homer, the "Iliad" and the "Odyssey," are foundational texts in Western literature. These works are filled with mythological characters and themes, chronicling the adventures of heroes like Achilles, Odysseus, and Hector. Homer's vivid storytelling set a high standard for narrative art, blending historical events with mythological elements to create timeless tales of heroism, honor, and tragedy.

Theater was another important medium for exploring mythological themes. Playwrights like Aeschylus, Sophocles, and Euripides used myths as the basis for their tragedies. Works such as "Oedipus Rex," "Medea," and "The Oresteia" delved into profound human emotions and moral dilemmas, drawing on well-known myths to engage audiences in deep reflection on ethical and existential issues.

Visual Arts

Greek mythology also heavily influenced visual arts in antiquity. Pottery, a ubiquitous aspect of daily life in ancient Greece, often featured intricate scenes from myths. Vases, bowls, and other ceramics depicted gods, heroes, and legendary events, serving both as decorative objects and as means of storytelling. These visual representations helped to keep myths alive in the public consciousness.

Sculpture and architecture were other prominent art forms where mythology played a crucial role. Temples dedicated to gods and goddesses were adorned with sculptures and friezes depicting mythological scenes. The Parthenon in Athens, for example, is decorated with sculptures that illustrate the birth of Athena and other mythological events. These artistic creations enhanced the aesthetic beauty of these structures and reinforced the cultural and religious significance of the myths.

Medieval and Renaissance Revival

The influence of Greek mythology persisted through the medieval period and saw a significant revival during the Renaissance. Artists and scholars of the Renaissance were fascinated by classical antiquity and sought to rediscover and reinterpret the myths of ancient Greece.

Literature

Renaissance writers such as Dante Alighieri, Geoffrey Chaucer, and William Shakespeare drew inspiration from Greek mythology. Dante's "Divine Comedy," while primarily a Christian allegory, incorporates classical elements and references to mythological figures like the Minotaur and Cerberus. Chaucer's "Canterbury Tales" includes allusions to Greek myths, reflecting the integration of these stories into the broader tapestry of European literature.

Shakespeare frequently referenced Greek mythology in his plays and sonnets. For instance, "A Midsummer Night's Dream" is infused with mythological elements, including the character of Theseus, the legendary king of Athens, and references to gods like Cupid and Diana.

Art

Renaissance artists, inspired by the classical ideals of beauty and harmony, created masterpieces that celebrated Greek mythology. Painters like Sandro Botticelli and sculptors like Michelangelo and Gian Lorenzo Bernini produced iconic works based on mythological themes. Botticelli's "The Birth of Venus" is a quintessential example, depicting the goddess Venus emerging from the sea. Michelangelo's sculptures, such as "Bacchus," and Bernini's dynamic "Apollo and Daphne" capture the dramatic and emotional essence of these ancient stories.

Modern Interpretations and Adaptations

Greek mythology continues to inspire contemporary art and literature, demonstrating its timeless appeal and relevance. Modern writers, filmmakers, and artists reinterpret these ancient stories, bringing new perspectives and creative energy to the myths.

Literature

Modern literature is replete with works that draw on Greek mythology. James Joyce's "Ulysses," a modernist retelling of the "Odyssey," is a prime example. Joyce's complex narrative parallels the adventures of Odysseus, transposed into the context of early 20th-century Dublin. Similarly, Margaret Atwood's "The Penelopiad" offers a feminist retelling of the "Odyssey" from Penelope's perspective, exploring themes of power, gender, and storytelling.

Rick Riordan's "Percy Jackson & the Olympians" series has introduced Greek mythology to a new generation of readers. By setting mythological adventures in the modern world, Riordan's books capture the imagination of young audiences and highlight the enduring relevance of these ancient stories.

Film and Television

Greek mythology has also made a significant impact on film and television. Classic films like "Jason and the Argonauts" and "Clash of the Titans" brought mythological tales to life with groundbreaking special effects. More recent adaptations, such as the "Percy Jackson" series and "Wonder Woman," which draws heavily on Greek myth, continue to captivate audiences with their dynamic retellings.

Television series like "Hercules: The Legendary Journeys" and "Xena: Warrior Princess" popularized mythological characters and adventures, blending ancient stories with modern sensibilities. These shows have helped keep Greek mythology alive in popular culture, introducing new audiences to the timeless tales.

Visual Arts

Contemporary artists continue to find inspiration in Greek mythology, exploring its themes and characters through various mediums. Paintings, sculptures, and installations often reinterpret mythological subjects, offering fresh perspectives and engaging with the myths in innovative ways.

Conclusion

The legacy of Greek mythology in art and literature is profound and far-reaching. From ancient epic poetry and drama to Renaissance masterpieces and modern adaptations, these myths have continually inspired creative expression across the ages. By exploring the influence of Greek mythology, we gain a deeper appreciation for its enduring impact and the timeless nature of these ancient stories. As we continue to reinterpret and engage with these myths, we ensure that their legacy lives on, enriching our cultural heritage and sparking our imaginations.

Greek mythology has a timeless quality that continues to captivate and inspire artists, writers, and creators in the modern era. The rich tapestry of gods, heroes, and epic tales offers a wealth of material that can be adapted and reimagined to resonate with contemporary audiences. From literature and film to television and digital media, modern interpretations and adaptations of Greek mythology breathe new life into these ancient stories.

Literature

Modern literature has embraced Greek mythology in various innovative ways, reinterpreting classic tales and exploring their themes through new lenses.

Novels and Retellings

Authors such as Madeline Miller have achieved great success with their novelistic retellings of Greek myths. Miller's "Circe" provides a fresh perspective on the life of the witch Circe, exploring her character in depth and giving voice to her struggles and triumphs. Similarly, her novel "The Song of Achilles" reimagines the story of Achilles and Patroclus, offering a nuanced exploration of their relationship and the events of the Trojan War.

Margaret Atwood's "The Penelopiad" retells the "Odyssey" from the perspective of Penelope, shedding light on her experiences and the lives of the maids who were hanged upon Odysseus's return. Atwood's feminist reinterpretation challenges traditional narratives and offers a new understanding of these characters.

Young Adult and Children's Literature

Rick Riordan's "Percy Jackson & the Olympians" series has introduced Greek mythology to a new generation of readers. By setting the adventures of demigods in the modern world, Riordan creates a compelling and relatable narrative for young audiences. The series combines humor, action, and mythology, making ancient stories accessible and engaging for today's youth.

Other authors, like Neil Gaiman in his book "Norse Mythology," although focusing on Norse myths, also incorporate elements of Greek mythology in their works, showcasing the interconnectedness of different mythological traditions and their impact on modern storytelling.

Film and Television

Greek mythology has long been a source of inspiration for filmmakers and television producers, leading to a variety of adaptations that bring these ancient stories to the screen.

Classic Films

Classic films such as "Jason and the Argonauts" (1963) and "Clash of the Titans" (1981) brought Greek myths to life with groundbreaking special effects and dramatic storytelling. These films captivated audiences with their epic scope and imaginative depictions of mythological creatures and gods.

Modern Blockbusters

Recent years have seen a resurgence of interest in Greek mythology in mainstream cinema. Films like "Troy" (2004), directed by Wolfgang Petersen, offer a cinematic retelling of the Trojan War, focusing on the characters of Achilles, Hector, and Helen. "Percy Jackson & the Olympians: The Lightning Thief" (2010) adapts Rick Riordan's popular book series, bringing the adventures of modern-day demigods to the big screen.

"Wonder Woman" (2017) and its sequel "Wonder Woman 1984" (2020), while primarily based on the DC Comics character, draw heavily on Greek mythology. The character of Diana Prince, or Wonder Woman, is depicted as an Amazonian princess with direct connections to the Greek gods, blending superhero and mythological genres.

Television Series

Television has also embraced Greek mythology, with series like "Hercules: The Legendary Journeys" and "Xena: Warrior Princess" becoming cult classics in the 1990s. These shows combined action, drama, and humor, reimagining mythological characters and stories for modern audiences.

More recently, Netflix's animated series "Blood of Zeus" (2020) offers a fresh take on Greek mythology, following a young hero's journey as he discovers his divine heritage and battles against demonic forces. The show blends traditional mythological elements with new narratives, creating an engaging and visually stunning experience.

Digital Media and Video Games

The influence of Greek mythology extends into digital media and video games, where interactive storytelling allows players to immerse themselves in mythological worlds.

Video Games

Games like "God of War" series (2005-present) have achieved immense popularity by incorporating Greek mythology into their narratives. Players control Kratos, a Spartan warrior who battles gods and monsters, exploring themes of vengeance, redemption, and the complexities of divine intervention.

"Assassin's Creed Odyssey" (2018) by Ubisoft transports players to ancient Greece during the Peloponnesian War, allowing them to interact with historical and mythological figures. The game combines historical accuracy with mythological elements, offering an immersive experience that brings ancient Greece to life.

Interactive Media

Interactive media, such as podcasts and web series, also explore Greek mythology in innovative ways. Podcasts like "Lore Olympus" reinterpret myths through modern storytelling techniques, blending humor, drama, and romance to engage contemporary audiences.

Conclusion

Modern interpretations and adaptations of Greek mythology demonstrate the enduring power and versatility of these ancient stories. Through literature, film, television, and digital media, creators continue to find new ways to engage with and reinterpret these myths, ensuring their relevance for future generations. By exploring these modern adaptations, we see how Greek mythology remains a vital and dynamic part of our cultural heritage, continually inspiring new forms of artistic expression and storytelling.

7.4 THE TALE OF ARACHNE

The tale of Arachne is a fascinating story from Greek mythology that explores themes of pride, skill, and the consequences of challenging the gods. Arachne, a talented weaver, dared to compare her skills to those of Athena, the goddess of wisdom and crafts. This myth not only highlights the importance of humility but also serves as a cautionary tale about the dangers of hubris.

The story of Arachne exemplifies how Greek myths have profoundly influenced cultural narratives and moral teachings. Arachne's tale illustrates the human tendency towards pride and the severe repercussions of overstepping boundaries set by the divine. It reflects ancient Greek values and provides a historical context for understanding how these myths were used to teach lessons and maintain societal norms. Moreover, Arachne's transformation into a spider also explains natural phenomena, showcasing the Greeks' way of integrating myths into their understanding of the world. By delving into this myth, we gain insight into the intricate ways Greek mythology continues to shape modern storytelling, art, and ethical considerations.

The Gifted Weaver

Arachne was a young woman from the region of Lydia, renowned for her extraordinary weaving skills. She came from a humble background, yet her talent was unmatched, and her creations were celebrated for their beauty and intricacy. People from all around admired her work, and her fame grew.

As her reputation spread, so did Arachne's pride. She began to boast that her weaving was superior to that of any mortal or deity, including Athena herself. This bold claim caught the attention of the goddess, who decided to confront Arachne and give her a chance to recant her boastful statements.

The Contest with Athena

Disguised as an old woman, Athena visited Arachne and warned her to be more humble and to acknowledge the gods' superiority. Arachne, unyielding and confident in her skills, dismissed the old woman's advice and reiterated her challenge. Revealing her true form, Athena accepted Arachne's challenge, and the contest began.

Each set up a loom and started weaving. Athena wove a tapestry that depicted the gods in their majestic glory, showcasing scenes of their power and benevolence. She included a warning against hubris, illustrating the fates of mortals who dared to defy the gods.

Arachne, on the other hand, chose to depict scenes that highlighted the gods' flaws and misdeeds. Her tapestry featured stories of gods disguising themselves to deceive mortals, such as

Zeus's numerous affairs. Arachne's work was undeniably beautiful and skillfully executed, but its content was provocative and irreverent.

The Transformation of Arachne

When the tapestries were completed, even Athena had to admit that Arachne's work was flawless. However, the content of Arachne's tapestry enraged the goddess. Unable to tolerate such insolence, Athena destroyed the tapestry and struck Arachne with her shuttle.

Devastated and humiliated, Arachne realized the gravity of her actions and, in despair, attempted to hang herself. Athena took pity on her, transforming Arachne into a spider instead of letting her die. This transformation allowed Arachne to continue weaving for eternity, but as a creature much lower in status.

Symbolism and Themes

The tale of Arachne is rich in symbolism and offers several important lessons:

1. **Hubris and Humility**: Arachne's downfall is a direct result of her hubris. By challenging a goddess and refusing to acknowledge her own limitations, Arachne brought about her own ruin. The story emphasizes the importance of humility and the dangers of excessive pride.
2. **Respect for the Gods**: Greek mythology often underscores the need to respect the gods and recognize their superior powers. Arachne's punishment serves as a reminder of the consequences of defying or disrespecting the divine.
3. **Transformation and Redemption**: Arachne's transformation into a spider can be seen as both a punishment and a form of redemption. While she loses her human form, she retains her weaving skills, albeit in a different context. This aspect of the story highlights themes of change and adaptation.

Personal Reflections on the Tale of Arachne

The story of Arachne resonates with me as a powerful reminder of the importance of humility and the perils of arrogance. One personal reflection that comes to mind is the idea that true mastery involves recognizing not only one's strengths but also one's limitations. Arachne's talent was undeniable, but her inability to temper her pride ultimately led to her downfall.

This myth also speaks to the value of respecting those who have come before us and acknowledging the sources of our inspiration and skills. In a world that often celebrates individual achievement, the tale of Arachne encourages us to remember the collective heritage and wisdom that contribute to our own successes.

Cultural Impact and Legacy

The tale of Arachne has had a lasting impact on literature, art, and popular culture. It has been retold and reinterpreted in various forms, from ancient texts to modern adaptations. The image of Arachne as a spider has become a symbol of intricate craftsmanship and the fine line between pride and humility.

In literature, the story has inspired numerous works, including poems, plays, and novels. For instance, Ovid's "Metamorphoses" vividly recounts Arachne's story, emphasizing the dramatic contest and her ultimate transformation. Artists have depicted the contest between Athena and Arachne in paintings, sculptures, and other visual arts, highlighting the dramatic tension and the transformative outcome of the myth. One notable example is Diego Velázquez's painting "Las Hilanderas" (The Spinners), which subtly references the myth through its depiction of weavers at work. These artistic and literary interpretations underscore the enduring legacy of Arachne's story, illustrating its timeless appeal and the powerful impact of Greek mythology on various forms of cultural expression.

Conclusion

The tale of Arachne is a compelling myth that explores themes of pride, skill, and divine retribution. Through her story, we learn about the importance of humility and the dangers of challenging the gods. As we continue to explore the influence of Greek mythology, the story of Arachne reminds us of the enduring power of these ancient tales to convey timeless lessons and inspire reflection on our own lives and actions.

7.5 THE STORY OF NIOBE

The story of Niobe is one of the most tragic and poignant tales in Greek mythology, highlighting themes of pride, punishment, and the consequences of defying the gods. Niobe, a queen known for her great pride and arrogance, suffers a devastating fate because of her hubris. This myth serves as a powerful reminder of the importance of humility and the peril of offending the divine.

The story of Niobe showcases how Greek mythology conveys moral lessons through deeply emotional and dramatic narratives. Niobe's tale emphasizes the severe consequences of excessive pride and disrespect towards the gods, reflecting the ancient Greek belief in maintaining reverence for the divine.

This myth provides a window into the cultural and religious values of ancient Greece and also illustrates the use of mythology to impart ethical teachings and social norms.

The Boast of Niobe

Niobe was the daughter of Tantalus, the king of Sipylus, and the wife of Amphion, the king of Thebes. She was blessed with numerous children, typically said to be fourteen—seven sons and seven daughters—though some versions of the myth mention different numbers. Niobe's large and beautiful family became a source of immense pride for her.

During a festival in honor of the goddess Leto, the mother of the twin gods Apollo and Artemis, Niobe made a grave mistake. She arrogantly boasted of her superiority over Leto, claiming that, as a mother of many children, she was far greater than Leto, who had only two. Niobe's pride and her disrespectful comparison angered Leto, who reported the insult to her divine children.

The Wrath of Apollo and Artemis

Apollo and Artemis, deeply offended by Niobe's hubris and her insult to their mother, decided to exact a terrible revenge. They descended to Thebes, determined to punish Niobe for her arrogance. With their divine powers, they swiftly and mercilessly carried out their retribution.

Apollo, the god of archery, targeted Niobe's sons. One by one, he shot them down with his arrows, leaving Niobe devastated and grief-stricken. Despite her pleas for mercy, the slaughter continued until all of her sons lay dead.

Artemis, the goddess of the hunt, turned her wrath on Niobe's daughters. Using her own arrows, she killed each of them, ignoring Niobe's desperate cries. In some versions of the myth, the youngest daughter is spared, but the overall result is the same: Niobe is left bereft of her children, her pride shattered by the overwhelming loss.

Niobe's Transformation

Overwhelmed by grief and remorse, Niobe fled to Mount Sipylus, her childhood home. There, she wept incessantly, her tears flowing without end. The gods, moved by her sorrow or perhaps as a final act of mercy, transformed Niobe into a stone. Even in this transformed state, the rock continued to weep, a perpetual symbol of her eternal mourning.

The image of the weeping stone on Mount Sipylus became a powerful symbol in Greek culture, representing the devastating consequences of hubris and the enduring nature of grief.

Symbolism and Themes

The story of Niobe is rich with symbolism and offers several important lessons:

1. **Hubris and Divine Retribution**: Niobe's downfall is a direct result of her excessive pride and disrespect toward the gods. Her story underscores the Greek belief that hubris, especially when directed at the divine, inevitably leads to severe punishment.
2. **The Power of the Gods**: The swift and decisive actions of Apollo and Artemis illustrate the immense power of the gods and their willingness to protect their honor and the honor of their family. This theme reinforces the importance of reverence and humility in the face of divine authority.
3. **Enduring Grief**: Niobe's transformation into a weeping stone symbolizes the enduring nature of grief and loss. Her eternal mourning serves as a poignant reminder of the profound impact of tragedy and the human capacity for sorrow.

Personal Reflections on the Story of Niobe

The story of Niobe resonates with me as a powerful cautionary tale about the dangers of arrogance and the importance of humility. One personal reflection that comes to mind is the idea that pride can blind us to the consequences of our actions, leading to devastating results. Niobe's inability to recognize the limits of her pride ultimately resulted in the loss of everything she held dear.

This myth also speaks to the universal experience of grief and the enduring impact of loss. Niobe's eternal mourning as a weeping stone is a vivid metaphor for the lasting nature of sorrow and the way it can shape our lives. Her story reminds us of the importance of empathy and compassion in the face of others' suffering.

Cultural Impact and Legacy

The story of Niobe has had a significant impact on art, literature, and culture throughout history. It has been depicted in various forms, from ancient Greek pottery and sculpture to Renaissance paintings and modern literary works. Artists have often portrayed the tragic moment of Niobe's loss or her transformation into the weeping stone, capturing the intense emotions and dramatic themes of the myth.

In literature, the tale of Niobe has been referenced by poets and writers such as Ovid, who included her story in his "Metamorphoses." The enduring themes of pride, punishment, and grief have made Niobe's story a compelling subject for artistic and literary exploration.

Conclusion

The story of Niobe is a poignant and tragic tale that explores themes of pride, divine retribution, and enduring grief. Through her story, we learn about the dangers of hubris and the profound consequences of offending the gods. The tale of Niobe reminds us of the timeless lessons these ancient myths offer and their ability to resonate with our own experiences and emotions.

7.6 SUMMARY AND KEY TAKEAWAYS

Summary

In this chapter, we explored the profound influence of Greek mythology on ancient Greek culture and its enduring legacy in art and literature. We examined how these myths have been reinterpreted and adapted in modern times, reflecting their timeless appeal and relevance.

We began with **Mythology in Ancient Greek Culture**, where we learned how myths were woven into the fabric of daily life, influencing religious practices, education, art, and social norms. Greek mythology provided a framework for understanding the world and imparting moral lessons, shaping the values and beliefs of ancient Greek society.

In **The Legacy of Greek Myths in Art and Literature**, we discussed how Greek mythology has inspired countless works of art and literature throughout history. From ancient epic poetry and drama to Renaissance masterpieces and modern adaptations, these myths have continually inspired creative expression across the ages.

Modern Interpretations and Adaptations highlighted how contemporary writers, filmmakers, and artists continue to draw on Greek mythology, reinterpreting these ancient stories to resonate with today's audiences. We explored examples from literature, film, television, and digital media, demonstrating the enduring impact of Greek mythology on popular culture.

We then delved into specific myths with **The Tale of Arachne** and **The Story of Niobe**. Arachne's tragic tale of hubris and divine retribution emphasizes the importance of humility and respect for the gods. Niobe's story, marked by pride and overwhelming grief, serves as a poignant reminder of the consequences of defying the divine and the enduring nature of sorrow.

Key Takeaways

Integration of Mythology in Daily Life

- Greek mythology was deeply integrated into ancient Greek culture, influencing religious practices, education, and social norms.
- Myths provided a common framework for understanding the world, imparting moral lessons, and shaping cultural identity.

Enduring Legacy in Art and Literature

- Greek mythology has inspired a vast body of art and literature, from ancient epic poems and plays to Renaissance paintings and modern novels.
- The themes and characters of Greek myths continue to resonate with audiences, reflecting universal human experiences and emotions.

Modern Adaptations and Reinterpretations

- Contemporary writers, filmmakers, and artists reinterpret Greek myths to address current themes and engage new audiences.
- Modern adaptations highlight the timeless appeal of these ancient stories and their relevance to contemporary issues.

Lessons from Specific Myths

- The tale of Arachne teaches the dangers of hubris and the importance of humility and respect for the gods.
- The story of Niobe underscores the consequences of excessive pride and the profound impact of grief and loss.

Reflective Questions

- How did Greek mythology shape the values and beliefs of ancient Greek society, and what lessons can we draw from this for our own culture?
- In what ways have modern adaptations of Greek myths made these ancient stories relevant to contemporary audiences?
- What do the tales of Arachne and Niobe teach us about the dangers of pride and the importance of humility in our own lives?

By exploring these questions, we can gain a deeper understanding of the enduring power of Greek mythology and its ability to inspire, educate, and resonate with people across different cultures and eras.

7.7 MYTHOLOGY QUIZ 7

Test your knowledge about the influence of Greek mythology on culture, art, and literature with the following questions:

1. **What role did Greek mythology play in ancient Greek daily life?**

    A) It was only used in children's stories.

    B) It influenced religious practices, education, and social norms.

    C) It was not significant in Greek culture.

    D) It was primarily used for political propaganda.

2. **Which ancient Greek poet is known for epic poems that feature mythological themes?**

    A) Sophocles

    B) Euripides

    C) Homer

    D) Aeschylus

3. **What was Arachne known for before her transformation?**

    A) Singing

    B) Dancing

    C) Weaving

    D) Painting

4. **How did modern author Madeline Miller reinterpret Greek mythology in her works?**

   A) By creating new gods

   B) By focusing on the lives and perspectives of lesser-known characters like Circe and Patroclus

   C) By setting the myths in outer space

   D) By writing them as historical accounts

5. **Which of these films is based on Greek mythology?**

   A) "The Lord of the Rings"

   B) "Harry Potter"

   C) "Clash of the Titans"

   D) "Star Wars"

6. **What is the main lesson from the tale of Arachne?**

   A) The importance of wealth

   B) The dangers of hubris and the importance of humility

   C) The need for adventure

   D) The value of physical strength

7. **What was Niobe's tragic mistake that led to her punishment by the gods?**

    A) She stole from the gods

    B) She boasted about her children being superior to those of Leto

    C) She tried to overthrow Zeus

    D) She refused to worship Apollo

8. **How have modern adaptations of Greek mythology made these ancient stories relevant to today's audiences?**

    A) By setting them in futuristic worlds

    B) By focusing on universal themes and reinterpreting the myths in contemporary contexts

    C) By eliminating the gods from the stories

    D) By making them entirely fictional

Note: Answers to the quiz can be found in the "Answer Key" section in the Appendix.

CHAPTER 8:
THE ENDURING LEGACY
OF GREEK MYTHOLOGY

Reflecting on the Myths

As we journey through the captivating world of Greek mythology, it's clear that these ancient stories are much more than mere tales of gods, heroes, and monsters. They are a profound exploration of human nature, societal values, and the complexities of life itself. Each myth, whether it recounts the bravery of Heracles, the cunning of Odysseus, or the tragedy of Niobe, offers timeless lessons and insights that continue to resonate with us today.

Reflecting on these myths, we see recurring themes such as the dangers of hubris, the importance of humility, the value of bravery, and the power of love and loyalty. These stories invite us to look within ourselves and our society, encouraging us to reflect on our own actions, beliefs, and values. They remind us that the struggles, triumphs, and moral dilemmas faced by the ancient Greeks are still relevant in our modern lives.

Greek mythology also highlights the rich tapestry of human experience. It addresses fundamental questions about existence, morality, and the human condition. By exploring these myths, we gain a deeper understanding of the universal truths that bind us across time and culture.

Continuing Your Mythological Journey

Our exploration of Greek mythology doesn't have to end here. There are countless ways to continue your journey and deepen your understanding of these fascinating stories and their impact on the world.

Reading and Research

Consider delving into original ancient texts such as Homer's "Iliad" and "Odyssey," Hesiod's "Theogony," and Ovid's "Metamorphoses." These works provide a wealth of mythological tales and are foundational to Western literature. Modern retellings, such as those by Madeline Miller or Rick Riordan, offer fresh perspectives and make these ancient stories accessible to contemporary readers.

Exploring Art and Media

Greek mythology has inspired a vast array of art, films, and television series. Visiting museums, exploring art galleries, and watching adaptations of these myths can provide new insights and appreciation for their cultural significance. Films like "Clash of the Titans" and "Wonder Woman," and series like "Blood of Zeus," bring these stories to life in visually stunning and engaging ways.

Participating in Discussions

Joining book clubs, online forums, or local mythology groups can enhance your understanding and enjoyment of Greek mythology. Discussing these myths with others allows you to share interpretations, learn from different perspectives, and deepen your appreciation for the stories.

Creating Your Own Interpretations

Engage with Greek mythology creatively by writing your own stories, poems, or plays inspired by these ancient myths. Drawing, painting, or crafting artworks based on mythological themes can also be a rewarding way to connect with these tales. Your interpretations and artistic expressions can help keep these stories alive and relevant for future generations.

Educational Opportunities

Consider taking courses on Greek mythology, whether through local universities, online platforms, or community education programs. These courses can provide structured learning and expert insights, enriching your understanding of the myths and their contexts.

Embracing the Mythological Spirit

Greek mythology offers a treasure trove of wisdom, inspiration, and entertainment. By reflecting on these ancient stories and continuing your mythological journey, you can discover new layers of meaning and relevance in your own life. Embrace the spirit of exploration, curiosity, and creativity that these myths inspire, and let them guide you on your own heroic journey through the world of imagination and beyond.

ACKNOWLEDGMENTS

Creating "Greek Mythology for Beginners" has been a journey filled with discovery, learning, and immense joy. This book would not have been possible without the support and contributions of many individuals.

First and foremost, I would like to express my deepest gratitude to my family and friends for their unwavering support and encouragement throughout this project. Your belief in me kept me motivated and inspired every step of the way.

I am also incredibly grateful to the scholars and writers whose works have laid the foundation for our understanding of Greek mythology. Their research and storytelling have provided invaluable insights and inspiration.

Special thanks to the talented illustrators who brought the gods, heroes, and mythical creatures to life through their beautiful and detailed artwork. Your creativity and dedication have added a vital dimension to this book, making it a richer experience for readers.

To my editor, thank you for your keen eye and thoughtful feedback, which have been crucial in shaping this book. Your expertise and guidance have greatly enhanced the quality of this work.

Finally, I want to extend my heartfelt appreciation to you, the readers. Your interest and enthusiasm for Greek mythology are what make this book meaningful. It is my hope that "Greek Mythology for Beginners" will ignite your imagination and deepen your understanding of these timeless stories.

Your Support Matters

Your feedback is incredibly valuable to us. Reviews help other readers discover this book and support its ongoing success. If you enjoyed "Greek Mythology for Beginners," please consider leaving a review. Your thoughts and insights not only help us improve but also enable others to embark on their own mythological journey.

APPENDIX

GLOSSARY OF TERMS

Achilles' Heel: A term originating from the myth of Achilles, referring to a person's point of greatest vulnerability.

Ambrosia: The food of the gods, believed to grant immortality to those who consumed it.

Apollo: The Greek god of the sun, music, poetry, and prophecy, son of Zeus and Leto, and twin brother of Artemis.

Arachne: A talented mortal weaver who challenged Athena and was transformed into a spider as punishment for her hubris.

Ares: The Greek god of war, son of Zeus and Hera, known for his fierce and aggressive nature.

Artemis: The Greek goddess of the hunt, wilderness, and childbirth, daughter of Zeus and Leto, and twin sister of Apollo.

Asphodel Meadows: A region of the Greek underworld where ordinary souls dwelled, neither particularly virtuous nor wicked.

Athena: The Greek goddess of wisdom, warfare, and crafts, often associated with the city of Athens, daughter of Zeus.

Cerberus: The three-headed dog that guards the entrance to the underworld, preventing the dead from leaving.

Charon: The ferryman of the underworld who transports souls across the River Styx in exchange for a coin placed in the mouth of the deceased.

Demeter: The Greek goddess of the harvest, agriculture, and fertility, mother of Persephone.

Dionysus: The Greek god of wine, festivity, and theater, son of Zeus and the mortal Semele.

Elysian Fields (Elysium): The paradisiacal part of the underworld reserved for heroes, the righteous, and those favored by the gods, where souls enjoy eternal happiness.

Erebus: A primordial deity representing darkness, born from Chaos.

Eros: The primordial god of love and attraction, often depicted as a young winged boy, representing the power of love and desire.

Furies: Deities of vengeance in Greek mythology, also known as the Erinyes, who punish crimes against the natural order.

Gaia: The primordial goddess of the Earth, mother of the Titans, and personification of the Earth itself.

Hades: The god of the underworld, brother of Zeus and Poseidon, and ruler of the dead.

Hephaestus: The Greek god of fire, metalworking, and craftsmanship, son of Hera, and husband of Aphrodite.

Hera: The queen of the gods, goddess of marriage and family, wife and sister of Zeus.

Hermes: The Greek god of travel, commerce, communication, and thieves, son of Zeus and the nymph Maia, and messenger of the gods.

Hestia: The Greek goddess of the hearth, home, and domesticity, one of the original twelve Olympians.

Hubris: Excessive pride or arrogance, often leading to a downfall, particularly in relation to defying the gods.

Minos, Rhadamanthus, and Aeacus: The three judges of the dead in the Greek underworld, who determine the fate of souls.

Nectar: The drink of the gods, often associated with granting immortality.

Niobe: A queen who boasted of her superior motherhood to Leto and was punished by having her children killed by Apollo and Artemis. She was transformed into a weeping stone.

Olympian Gods: The principal deities in Greek mythology who reside on Mount Olympus, including Zeus, Hera, Poseidon, Demeter, Athena, Apollo, Artemis, Ares, Aphrodite, Hephaestus, Hermes, and Dionysus.

Pandora's Box: A mythological artifact containing all the evils of the world, which were released when Pandora opened the box, leaving only hope inside.

Persephone: The daughter of Demeter, abducted by Hades to become the queen of the underworld. Her annual return to the earth represents the changing seasons.

Poseidon: The Greek god of the sea, earthquakes, and horses, brother of Zeus and Hades.

Prometheus: A Titan who defied Zeus by giving fire to humanity, symbolizing foresight and the pursuit of knowledge.

River Styx: The river in the underworld that forms the boundary between the living and the dead. Gods swore oaths by the Styx, which were considered unbreakable.

Sisyphus: A king condemned to an eternal punishment of rolling a boulder up a hill, only for it to roll back down each time he neared the summit, symbolizing futile labor.

Tantalus: A mortal punished in the underworld by standing in a pool of water under a fruit tree, forever unable to drink or eat, for his crimes against the gods.

Tartarus: The deepest part of the underworld where the wicked and the enemies of the gods are punished.

Thetis: A sea nymph and mother of Achilles, who dipped him into the River Styx to make him nearly invulnerable.

Uranus: The primordial god of the sky, husband of Gaia, and father of the Titans.

Zeus: The king of the gods, ruler of Mount Olympus, and god of the sky, thunder, and justice.

RECOMMENDED READING

Classical Texts:

1. **"The Iliad" by Homer**: An epic poem detailing the events of the Trojan War and the heroics of Achilles.
2. **"The Odyssey" by Homer**: Follow Odysseus's long journey home after the fall of Troy.
3. **"Theogony" by Hesiod**: A comprehensive genealogy of the Greek gods.
4. **"Metamorphoses" by Ovid**: A narrative poem that includes many mythological transformations.

Modern Retellings:

5. **"Circe" by Madeline Miller**: A novel exploring the life of Circe, the enchantress from the Odyssey.
6. **"The Song of Achilles" by Madeline Miller**: A reimagining of the relationship between Achilles and Patroclus.
7. **"Mythos" by Stephen Fry**: A modern retelling of Greek myths with humor and wit.
8. **"The Penelopiad" by Margaret Atwood**: A retelling of the Odyssey from Penelope's perspective.

Reference Books:

9. **"D'Aulaires' Book of Greek Myths" by Ingri and Edgar Parin d'Aulaire**: A classic illustrated collection of Greek myths for all ages.
10. **"Mythology: Timeless Tales of Gods and Heroes" by Edith Hamilton**: A comprehensive guide to Greek, Roman, and Norse mythology.
11. **"The Greek Myths" by Robert Graves**: A detailed and scholarly collection of Greek myths, exploring their origins and meanings.

RESOURCES FOR FURTHER STUDY

Online Databases and Libraries:

- **Perseus Digital Library**: A comprehensive resource for classical texts and translations.
  URL: http://www.perseus.tufts.edu/

- **Theoi Greek Mythology**: An extensive site covering the gods, spirits, and heroes of Greek mythology.
  URL: https://www.theoi.com/

- **Project Gutenberg**: Offers free access to many classical texts, including works by Homer and Hesiod.
  URL: https://www.gutenberg.org/

Educational Platforms:

- **Coursera**: Offers courses on Greek mythology and ancient Greek culture from top universities.
  URL: https://www.coursera.org/

- **edX**: Provides courses on Greek history and mythology, often free to audit.
  URL: https://www.edx.org/

Museums and Exhibitions:

- **The British Museum**: Hosts an extensive collection of Greek artifacts and provides online resources and virtual tours.
  URL: https://www.britishmuseum.org/

- **The Acropolis Museum**: Offers insights into ancient Greek history and mythology through its collections and online resources.
  URL: https://www.theacropolismuseum.gr/en

Journals and Publications:

- **Classical Journal**: Publishes scholarly articles on Greek and Roman antiquity.
  URL: https://classicalstudies.org/publications-and-research/classical-journal

- **Hesperia**: A journal focusing on Greek archaeology, history, and literature.
  URL: https://www.ascsa.edu.gr/publications/hesperia

Online communities:

Reddit:

1. **r/GreekMythology**: A subreddit dedicated to discussions about Greek mythology, including myths, gods, and historical context.
   URL: https://www.reddit.com/r/GreekMythology/

2. **r/Mythology**: A broader subreddit that covers various mythologies from around the world, including Greek mythology.
   URL: https://www.reddit.com/r/Mythology/

Other Platforms:

3. **Mythology and Folklore Stack Exchange**: A Q&A site where you can ask questions and share knowledge about Greek mythology and other mythologies.
   URL: https://mythology.stackexchange.com/

4. **Facebook Groups**: There are several Facebook groups dedicated to Greek mythology where enthusiasts can share information and discuss various topics. Simply search "Greek Mythology" in the Facebook search bar to find these

communities.

5. **Goodreads**: There are discussion groups and book clubs focused on Greek mythology. Members share book recommendations, discuss interpretations, and explore various myths.

   URL: https://www.goodreads.com/group (Search for Greek mythology within the groups section)

ANSWER KEY

Mythology Quiz 1 Answers:

1. B) Chaos
2. C) Gaia and Uranus
3. B) Swallowed them at birth
4. C) Metis
5. C) Fire
6. C) All the evils of the world
7. C) Hope

Mythology Quiz 2 Answers:

1. B) Hestia
2. C) Hermes
3. A) Poseidon
4. C) Artemis
5. C) Ares
6. B) Athena
7. D) Hephaestus

Mythology Quiz 3 Answers:

1. C) Ariadne
2. A) A sword and a shield
3. B) Medea
4. B) A she-bear
5. B) Hubris
6. B) By having his men tie him to the mast

Mythology Quiz 4 Answers:

1. C) Perseus
2. B) By burning the neck stumps
3. A) It had three heads: a lion, a goat, and a serpent

4. D) Polyphemus
5. C) They had the upper body of a human and the lower body of a horse
6. B) Chiron
7. B) By strangling it with his bare hands
8. C) What walks on four legs in the morning, two legs at noon, and three legs in the evening?
9. B) He answered its riddle correctly
10. B) The lion's own claws

Mythology Quiz 5 Answers:

1. B) Orpheus had to not look back at Eurydice until they reached the surface.
2. D) A beautiful wife as perfect as his statue.
3. B) She was cursed by Hera to only repeat the words of others.
4. D) He starved to death, entranced by his own reflection.
5. A) A pomegranate.
6. C) Through a crack in the wall between their houses.
7. C) They were transformed into intertwined trees.

Mythology Quiz 6 Answers:

1. C) Hades
2. B) The boundary between the living and the dead
3. C) Charon
4. B) Eternal bliss and paradise
5. C) Tartarus
6. B) Rolling a boulder up a hill, only for it to roll back down each time
7. C) For murdering his son and serving him to the gods
8. C) Standing in a pool of water under a fruit tree, forever unable to drink or eat

Mythology Quiz 7 Answers:

1. B) It influenced religious practices, education, and social norms.
2. C) Homer
3. C) Weaving
4. B) By focusing on the lives and perspectives of lesser-known characters like Circe and Patroclus
5. C) "Clash of the Titans"
6. B) The dangers of hubris and the importance of humility
7. B) She boasted about her children being superior to those of Leto
8. B) By focusing on universal themes and reinterpreting the myths in contemporary contexts

Made in the USA
Las Vegas, NV
23 December 2024

15297419R00154